BIG SHOES

ALSO BY JACK GETZE

Austin Carr Mysteries
Big Numbers
Big Money
Big Mojo

JACK GETZE

BIG SHOES

An Austin Carr Mystery

Down & Out Books
3959 Van Dyke Rd, Ste. 265
Lutz, FL 33558
www.DownAndOutBooks.com

Cover design by JT Lindroos

ISBN: 1943402051
ISBN-13: 978-1-943402-05-2

For my big brother Mike

ONE

The big thing about my temporary business partner, Angelina "Mama Bones" Bonacelli: her routine professional consultations can easily deteriorate into criminal activity and violence. Breakfast appointments have been raided by the FBI. Her Power Point presentation to a Jersey state racing commission last summer ended in a fist fight, then later in the parking lot, automatic weapons fire. As a Jersey shore racketeer with direct ties to what's left of a once powerful New York crime family, Mama Bones packs an abundance of local power, not to mention a loaded nine-millimeter.

For me, Austin Carr, mild-mannered bond salesman, our association has been terrifyingly problematic. Bullets, knives and poison keep turning up at mutually occupied locations and joint functions. In fact, I am lucky to be alive—charmed, really—and I've decided I need a new temporary partner or a new livelihood. Trying to explain these concerns to Mama Bones last month, following the funeral of one Heriberto Garzia, a man murdered before my eyes, Mama Bones told me to take a vacation. Think about my future, she said. Don't rush into drastic change. Maybe when Vic gets better you'll feel different, she said. Not likely. Her son Vic— my real business partner, who Mama Bones is subbing for—remains physically wounded and mentally unstable following an earlier, unrelated shootout. Unrelated except that minutes before being shot, both gunshot victims—Heriberto and Vic—were talking to me.

I did take several weeks off, per Mama Bones' strong suggestion, but the results are not what she'd hoped. An exhaustive detailing of past events and stern logic worked against her, particularly a list I made of her associates, men either murdered or who disappeared over the past three years. There weren't *that* many names. Okay. But it was a list. Honestly, only a suicidal fool would stay. So this morning, Wednesday, June 25, my vacation is over. I'm here to tell Mama Bones the bad news: Bonacelli Investments will have to do without me. I've sold my last tax-free bond.

I avoid a doublewide trailer set hastily on concrete blocks in our back lot, then park my black Toyota Solara near our brick building's rear entrance. Some Cadillac SUV owner has taken my spot, a white-outlined space that says RESERVED is big blue letters. Must be some meth head. I'm no big shot, I'm Austin Carr, chairman and fifty-one percent owner of Bonacelli Investments, formerly Carr Securities, a regional brokerage firm. We only have one office. We sell stocks, bonds, mutual funds and the kind of insurance that wraps around investment products.

Inside my firm's back office, key employees Jerry and Pat welcome my return with muted celebration. They wave. "What's with that trailer out back?" I say. "The thing is taking up half our parking."

"Ask Mama Bones," Jerry says.

Great. "Is she here this morning?"

"No," Jerry says. "She's still down at the diner." He glances at his large stack of paperwork, then back up at me. "She hasn't been coming in until after lunch. And before you raise a stink in front of the salesmen, you better know that's Gianni's Escalade in your reserved parking spot."

Gianni Rossi. Mama Bones' nephew, bodyguard and pistol-packing crime lieutenant. Probably next in line to her illegal gambling throne. Looks like I must resign myself to another small humiliation.

"Is Gianni here?" I ask.

"He's with Mama Bones at the diner."

Mama Bones now owns Branchtown's landmark Pardon Me Diner, strategically situated across Monmouth Street from our municipal courthouse and police headquarters. Four blocks from our offices. I wave to my friends and newer brokers in the big sales room on the way, but I'm out the front door and down the street in fifteen seconds, passing on the way another of Mama Bones' centrally-located businesses, Domenic's Bail Bonds.

Not many people walking on the sidewalks of Branchtown this late in the morning. A few shoppers. We had an unusually cold and snow-filled winter with lots of snow days, and the kids are in class through the end of June. The streets will be more crowded next week, and packed for the Fourth of July.

Inside the diner, I don't bother asking directions, remembering where the diner's old office was. I discover Mama Bones behind the closed door next to the Pardon Me's newly expanded kitchen. Vic told me his mother was born in 1945, which makes her seventy years old this year, but she's exercising briskly on a tread mill as I barge in. Mama Bones wears leopard-patterned leotards. Jeez, she's neither flabby nor weak as I imagined. More stocky and hard.

From his seat on a plastic-covered orange couch, Gianni Rossi aims a shotgun at me. He's wearing tan shorts and a gorgeous blue Tommy Bahama camp shirt, acting all business, however, racking a shell into the pump-action weapon, ready to blow off my head despite having known me for years. Or maybe *because* he's known me for years. I once rescued him from an electric meat smoker. Maybe that will help.

Mama Bones glares at me as she flips off the NordicTrack. "You don't knock?"

"Sorry," I say. "I wasn't sure you were in here."

"All the more reason, Smarty Pants."

Mama Bones always wears ankle-length black dresses. There's one draped over the back of the swivel desk chair. Like her Italian accent, the simple garb is designed to make her appear weak, maybe out of touch, when in fact Mrs. Angelina Bonacelli—a widow since 1994—is tougher than week-old tomato pie.

"I wanted you to know as soon as I made up my mind," I say. "I'm not coming back to work at Bonacelli Investments. I'm done."

Mama Bones hops off the treadmill, wraps a beach towel around her shoulders and chest, then hurries to hide behind a cherry wood desk that matches the woodwork on the orange couch. "I'm glad you're back," she says. "I can't spend no more time running Vic's business. I got too many problems."

I shake my head. "Mama Bones, didn't you hear me? I said I'm done. I've given it a lot of thought, careful consideration like you suggested, but I need to quit. Heriberto being killed in front of me changed things. Forever. I can't take the violence. Luis agrees with me. He said he would talk to you."

Luis Guerrero is more than my closest friend. In this context, and many times before in my life, the bartender and owner of Luis' Mexican Grill is my spiritual advisor. Luis was not a witness to Heriberto's murder at the racetrack, but he was on the scene soon after, showing up in time to see the murderer—a gangster called the Turk—and help me safely get away. That wasn't the first time Luis saved my life.

Mama Bones glances toward Gianni. "You hungry?"

"I could eat," he says.

I get the feeling Mama Bones is not taking me seriously.

She brings her dark eyes back to mine. "We need to talk. How 'bout some lunch?"

"Mama Bones, I need you to under—"

She waves her hand. "You are not walking away from Vic's investment business today or tomorrow, okay? Maybe next week. Maybe next month. But not today. He needs you. And I need you. Vic ran away from the rehab hospital. Nobody can find him." She scowls at Gianni. "And a bad fire chased my friends into that trailer you saw. Plus Johnny the Turk Korsay is on some kind-a rampage, had his crooked cops arrest Luis."

"Arrest Luis?" I say. "For what?"

"For Heriberto's murder, what do you think, huh?"

"But the Turk killed Heriberto. I saw him."

"Yeah, and that's why those crooked cops probably gonna come after you next."

Gianni and I slide into the big corner booth at the Pardon Me Diner minutes later, order menus and a pot of coffee. Mama Bones will dress and join us. Our view across the restaurant's eating area and through the floor-to-ceiling windows is primarily of Branchtown's municipal courthouse. Across Main Street, the century-old gray building sports Roman columns and marble steps, but also stands alongside Mr. Basil's Hot Dog Shack, Mr. Basil and his wife Becky taking customers' money through a cut-out slot in a six-foot red wiener. The whole city is like that, a hodge-podge of old and new, fancy and poor, bright paint and weather-worn marble façades. For me, Branchtown's ancient and eclectic architecture conjures old brown and white photographs of America during the 1930s and our Great Depression.

I get tired of the silence. "So how did Mama Bones end up with the Pardon Me Diner?"

Gianni's gaze stays on the front door. "Before the previous owner skipped bail eight years ago, he mortgaged the place to Mama Bones," he says. "You remember Croc Tierney, our ex-mayor? Spent his bribe money at the racetrack?"

"Yeah. He was indicted with all those other Jersey mayors, zoning commissioners and rabbis, right? That FBI sting on construction bids, zoning changes. I remember because there were charges of organ selling, too, and that made national TV."

"Whatever," Gianni says, "Croc made payments to Mama Bones for years through a numbered account in Panama, but they stopped. Croc probably figured the property wasn't worth what he owed."

"I can tell she likes the place."

Gianni nods. "Yeah, she figures the location will help her bail bond business."

"A free meal with every bond?"

"Including dessert and beverage."

Gianni and I smile, but indeed the Pardon Me Diner throbs with customers. Nice menus, too, the back cover featuring a story about her family and a black and white, high school photograph of a young Mama Bones, her dark eyes and creamy skin in a strikingly pretty, three-quarter profile. She's wearing a starched white blouse with an exaggerated man's collar like an old movie star from the middle of last century. Maybe Natalie Wood in *Rebel Without A Cause.*

Speak of the Devil. Dressed now in her all black widow's outfit, Mama Bones catches me and Gianni still smirking over her marketing plans. She folds her arms across her chest, poses standing above our table, scowling like a school principal, her two faces side by side before me—one from the past on a menu, the now-face here live—producing a tender portrait of aging. Mama Bones' basic Mediterranean beauty still holds a permanent grip.

"If you two smarty pants are through making jokes," she says, "maybe we could figure out what we're gonna do about Luis, four homeless women and the Turk."

"What homeless women?" I ask.

"My friends in the trailer."

I nod like her information makes sense. "How's Vic? Before he disappeared, I mean. Was he getting better?"

Mama Bones slides into the booth next to Gianni and glares at him again. "Vic is gonna be okay. He says he's confused about life, but who isn't, huh? This crazy world. But Vic is more than confused. He's acting like a mamaluke, dressing up, giving speeches. Last weekend we found him at Branchtown High School talking to an assembly."

"I have everyone looking," Gianni says. "Everybody."

"Vic is gonna be fine," she says. "My problem, yours, too, Austin Carr, is the Turk. He's mad that I know he shot Heriberto, mad because Luis called me that night, not the police like he told you. That makes me the one who got Turk out of his jam. I sent his favorite two cops, Davenport and Lindsay, to pick him up, but he's worried I'll use the information against him, I guess. Maybe with New York. Also, what I hear, the Turk thinks you saw something that night which could hurt him."

"I saw him murder Heriberto," I say. "What's worse than that?"

"I don't know. But he doesn't worry about Heriberto no more. The report those two cops filed says they found Heriberto's body in the trunk of an abandoned car, so there's no investigation of the Turk. And now those two cops grabbed Luis, trying to frame him, or wanting to know why Luis called me that night. The Turk asking questions through the cops."

I'm impressed with Mama Bones' knowledge, and frankly wonder at her sources of information. I can see why my mentally unstable and currently missing partner Mr. Vic thinks his mother sometimes reads minds.

"You gonna ask how come I know so much police business?" she asks.

What? How could...

"We know lots of cops," Gianni says. "Including Davenport and Lindsay. Both are Lieutenants in the Seaside County Prosecutor's Gambling Enterprises Unit. Turk pays them more, but they're also on Mama Bones' payroll. Or extortion list, whatever you want to call it."

I am not soothed. In fact, I am washed over by another wave of discomfort. I should not ask questions the answers to which I do not want to hear. That inside trading investigation last year taught me there are pieces of intelligence it's best not to collect. Then again, Mama Bones and Gianni didn't need to explain how they know so much. They both volunteered a lot. I worry something's going on.

"How come you're telling me all this?" I ask. "I know I kind of asked, but this is your...uh...family business stuff. I'm an outsider."

Mama Bones shakes her head. "Not no more, Smarty Pants. Until Vic gets better and can run that bond shop again, you gotta work for me. Me and my homeless friends need your help."

Gianni smiles from inside that spectacular Tommy

Bahama camp shirt, his calm manner a visual underlining of Mama Bones' words. In fact, Gianni's confident grin is more formidable than the shotgun.

TWO

Angelina Rossi—later to become Mama Bones Bonacelli—grew up five miles south of Branchtown in the summer resort of Asbury Park. Her parents leased special soda-making equipment and illegal betting cards to venders on the Jersey shore, a business begun in the 1920s by her grandparents, Giuseppe and Francesca Rossi. Grandma and Grandpa were also political organizers, collecting cash from new Italian immigrants and boardwalk businesses, then delivering the bag money plus ninety percent of the local Italian vote to whichever party paid them most. In short, Mama Bones' family has been a community leader for the past century, three generations of royalty in the politically-established, highly profitable and still shady Jersey shore tourist industry. And while it is true Mama Bones saved my life several times, the most recent occasion involved only a last minute change of heart, her outlaw hand on a switch that could have ground me into mincemeat.

I'm not sure I owe her any favors.

Still, the jailed Luis Guerrero is as close to me as an older brother, a guiding hand whenever my grip on life grows shaky, and now the hombre needs my help. I can't and won't run away from Luis if he needs me. Also, there is Mama Bones' desires to consider, not to mention Gianni's smile and his shotgun. Weighing all options and potential consequences, I believe it best my departure from the stock and bond business be temporarily delayed.

"So," I say. "What's the plan?"

The Pardon Me Diner hums with conversation and

the clatter of racking dishes. Mama Bones sips her black coffee. "Go back to Vic's bond shop, sell bonds," she says. "Wait for me or Gianni to call. First thing, we gotta get Luis out of jail—or at least away from those two cops. I called his lawyer—that guy Zimmer you know—and he's working on bail. But he told me Luis was moved from the Seaside County lockup. Zimmer was having trouble finding him."

"They're corrupt cops, but cops," I say. "They wouldn't kill him, would they?"

Mama Bones lifts her beefy shoulders. "I'm not so sure."

"We need leverage," Gianni says. "How about we threaten to turn Austin over to the Feds unless the Turk releases Luis?"

Mama Bones' face wrinkles into a living walnut shell. "Go to the cops? New York would probably kill us first." She sighs. "I should have known Turk wouldn't trust me. When Luis called me that night, I should have made somebody else send those two cops to the racetrack, somebody I could trust not to tell."

Mama Bones refers to a cell phone call Luis Guerrero made to her this past May from the racetrack—the site of Heriberto's murder—and Mama Bones' subsequent calls to get her capo the Turk out of trouble. I'd gone to the track's backside, or stable area that night on the spur of the moment, accompanying Heriberto who claimed to be meeting a horse trainer. The trainer turned out to be the Turk, who shot Heriberto, calling him a juicer—a chemist who supplies drugs to make horses run faster and longer, or drugs to mask the initial drug. The Turk would have killed me, too, but an angry horse and Luis saved my life. It was a crazy night, one that taught me plenty about my big mouth. Another thing I remember, another reason the Turk was angry—the Turk said

Heriberto had stolen his woman at a party. A redhead.

"We make the threat like it doesn't come from us," Gianni says, "We get someone else to lay it out for Turk's lawyer, maybe that DEA agent we know."

Mama Bones shrugs. "I don't like it...but maybe if we can trust the DEA to say the request comes from Luis' family or something."

"What about the redhead Heriberto supposedly stole from Turk at the Turk's own party?" I say. "She could testify the Turk had another motive for killing Heriberto. Put her and myself together, you have a strong case, not only against the Turk, but those county cops as well, Davenport and Lindsay, for hiding Turk's guilt."

Gianni nods. "That sounds like leverage to me. We threaten the Turk with Austin *and* the redhead. Make Turk's lawyer believe the threat comes from Luis' family. Hell, we can probably get Luis' wife to accompany the DEA agent."

"Might work," Mama Bones says. "Solana will definitely help. She's already called me."

"But do we even know who the redhead is?" I ask.

"Solana heard it was Croc Tierney's daughter," Mama Bones says. "Name's Emma. She lives in Rumson with Croc's sister, a horsey-type named Barbara Ryder. Ryder fixed her brother's business problems after Croc skipped bail. She handled the Pardon Me mortgage, in fact, bought me lunch at Clooney's the day we signed the papers. She complained about her daughter back then. Redheaded, pretty and spoiled."

"Turk loves the ponies, owns a stable of them," Gianni says. "He's always at the track. If Emma's aunt is another horse owner, it adds up."

Mama Bones nods. "This Emma Tierney also has a reputation for crazy, Solana says—*pazzo* enough to date the Turk and then dump him at his own party."

"Can we find out for sure?" I ask.

"I'll check it out," Mama Bones says, "reconnect with this Barbara Ryder. If it sounds like Emma's the right one, I'll set something up for you to meet her, get her feelings on helping us. You're the redhead expert, right? You busy this weekend?"

Excuse me, but I do not understand the widespread popularity of Asian restaurants with searing hot, ping pong table sized griddles. Those flame-throwing onion towers have been known to burn off beards and eyebrows. Forget about the teenage chefs juggling razor-sharp cleavers, blades that could bleed you out before an ambulance arrived. Restaurants should be about serving food, not threatening customers' mortality.

Most people don't see it that way, apparently, as Taki's in Branchtown hums with Sunday evening customers. Young and old are packed shoulder to shoulder in a bamboo forest, lined up around frying meat and vegetables. Emma Tierney is one of the forty or fifty diners who enjoy this menace while they eat. I find her perched in a corner at the last of Taki's eight hibachi grills, Emma talking to her date, a wiry and taut Russian-looking guy who probably was born in Newark. Whatever, he stares at me with hazel eyes too small for his face. Head shaved, his skin so pale and pocked, I can't help thinking of a full moon. My internal alarms vibrate.

"Ms. Tierney?" I say.

Emma swivels her attention from Full Moon to assess me. Heriberto's alleged mistress certainly matches the description Heriberto gave me that night on the way to the racetrack. Her wine-red hair shines in dark, long waves. Her pale white skin glows under a feline canopy of freckled spots.

"You must be Austin," she says.

"Yes, ma'am. Nice to meet you."

"Do you mind waiting in the bar?" she says. "I'll be finished here in ten or fifteen minutes."

Already tingling from the proximity of Full Moon, a guy who I sense wants to kill me, my spine shudders with an electric tremor. Like the odd lightning strike, I can't tell if this new charge started at the bottom and rose, or began at the top then fell. What I do know, Emma Tierney's voice, her manner and word choices do not please my instincts. A strong flame of resentment blossoms inside me. She wants me to go wait somewhere else? Beyond her queenly presence? For ten or fifteen minutes? Seems a bit rude. For Luis, however, I will proceed. All I have to do tonight is introduce myself, ask her to meet with the DEA agent and Gianni. I draw a slow breath and give Emma Tierney the full-boat Carr grin. While I don't expect my smile to warm up this frosty glass of cherry soda, the Austin Carr Full Boat Grin is always worth a shot. Sometimes, my charm even surprises myself.

"Are you deaf?" Emma says. "Or just dumb?"

A spear lances my heart. Full Moon chuckles out loud. His teeth are yellowed from cigarettes and coffee. The smell of tobacco harbors in his clothes. And while Emma at least now stays silent, her smile is so sad and condescending, my hands clench. Wow. I am normally so easy-going I fail to recognize most insults. Ninety-nine percent of the slanders I do perceive, I choose to ignore. But once in a while—maybe half a dozen times in my whole life—somebody says something I find so insulting, a switch snaps. My gift of gab turns ugly and mean. Am I deaf—or just dumb? I can't believe anyone would say that to me, especially a pretty woman. Or maybe it's not her words at all. Maybe this rising bile of hatred awash in my belly is the result of Emma's nasty, puke-on-you smile. My neck is as hot as a Costa Rican beach.

I show Emma another grin, this one displaying real teeth. "Does your date know you like to hump stable boys at Seaside Park?"

That wipes out the redhead's smile and her date's chuckle. Also, of course, I'm immediately embarrassed. Losing my temper is a lousy excuse for generally insulting women, stable boys and a significant Seaside County institution where famed thoroughbreds occasionally roam. As has been pointed out to me before, I have a big mouth. At times, completely unfiltered. Obviously, ancient, subconscious and unwelcome prejudices occasionally bubble up when I'm angry.

Emma hisses. The wrath flashing from Miss Tierney's blue eyes suggests Heriberto's story was true—she did have sex with him. And while I figure my interview with Emma Tierney tonight is over—she's reaching for her hot Japanese tea—I've at least confirmed the redhead's relevance as a potential source for leverage against the Turk. Emma could tell the cops plenty about Heriberto and events immediately prior to his murder. Particularly that private party where she ditched the Turk.

Full Moon stands, shows me how much taller he is. Maybe an inch. But strategically more important, and something I worry about far more, Full Moon carries, shifts and steadies his weight like my friend Luis—that is, with extreme ease, balance and athleticism.

Sensing the intended discharge of Emma's scalding liquid, and the boiling stuff's future location—my face— I leap sideways. What my English grandmother might have called a spot of tea catches my wrist, but the bulk of hot liquid splashes onto the floor. Distracted, however, I fail to sense the arrival of strange hands and arms before they clamp me motionless from behind. I'm startled, defusing my efforts to resist. A thick elbow slips around my throat and pulls me backward. I'm immobilized.

So much has happened so quickly, the events so threatening, my brain has pretty much ceded control to my medulla oblongata—that is, the lowest portion, or so-called lizard brain, which deals only with basic functions like breathing. Instinct. And though I am now ready to choke, kick, punch and kill, I never get the chance. While I am helpless in another man's grip, Full Moon punches the side of my head. My vision turns into a science show, dark stars circling red and yellow suns.

I'm thrown against the giant grill and crash to the floor, ribs burning. I lash out with my right foot, but succeed only in bringing the chef's cooking cart down on top of me. Surprised voices and the clatter of equipment circle me like hungry birds.

"Pick him up."

My neck gets swallowed by a big hand. I am forced to rise and walk forward or have my head ripped off. Full Moon and his unknown assistant hustle me through Taki's hibachi grill like I couldn't pay my bill, or I'm an accused Ponzi-schemer doing the perp walk. The guy strangling me wears a yellow golf shirt.

While I am inspected by half a dozen strangers, Taki's heavy double doors slowly part to reveal a new would-be guest. Oh my. I'm sure I know this costumed person, but my brain is always slow when processing strange information. The image is a puzzle. I recognize the purple trim on his white toga, the classic Roman nose, but he can't be a Senator from the time of Julius Caesar. No, it's my business partner, Vic Bonacelli, Mama

Bones' missing son, dressed in a purple-trimmed bed sheet. Poor Vic. Will our best bond salesman ever recover from last year's gunshot-induced health problems?

"Release the barbarian to me," Vic says. "He has stolen my wealth."

Vic apparently doesn't know his mother re-established family ownership of our mutual business, my controlling shares having been contracted to Mr. Vic while Mama Bones held my life in her hands. Even less surprising, Full Moon does not give a flying duck what Mr. Vic thinks or says. Full Moon lets go of my arm to punch Vic and wrestle him to the restaurant floor.

This guy with pock marks all over his face likes to hit people, I guess.

The Russian's move was violent and quick, but so am I when required. I take advantage of Full Moon's diverted attention by stomping with all my force on the exposed knee of the guy in the yellow golf shirt. He screams in pain and tumbles to the floor, joining the squirming pile of flesh and bed sheet that is Full Moon and my partner. Hey, look at Mr. Vic wrestle.

The customers think fighting is part of the show. I earn modest applause running toward the kitchen.

Outside, I reach for my cell phone. Mama Bones needs to hear about Vic.

Angelina Bonacelli earned her nickname one year after marrying her husband Domenic Bonacelli, a crime family soldier. What they used to call a made man. He was too handsome to resist, she told her friends. It was 1965, and her man Domenic's world of organized crime was still influential, prosperous and sometimes violent. Domenic had invited his wife to meet for dinner after work, and at their favorite sidewalk cafe, two druggies tried to steal the brown paper shopping bag of cash Domenic had collected earlier from bookies. He would tell the hospital nurses he shouldn't have held the cash while eating with his wife, but that evening he had, and the two heroin addicts drew pistols and demanded the money. Twenty years old and a bit impulsive, Angelina interfered, throwing her drink at the closest thief. For her effort she earned a gun-smack to the forehead, and awarded her husband a bullet in the thigh. But Asbury Park High School's former prom queen recovered to aid her wounded husband. Knocked to her knees, she secretly snagged Domenic's revolver from his coat pocket and shot both addicts as they argued over the bag, Angelina seriously wounding one and killing the other. She was seven months pregnant at the time with Vic's older sister Mary, and Angelina's swelling belly earned her double the respect of Domenic and his friends in the New York family. What in those days they called a condition also justified their new nickname for her— Mama Bones.

Tonight, wondering how she will handle so many problems at once, the widow of Domenic Bonacelli rests in her favorite wicker lawn chair on her Branchtown home's wrap-around porch, a cool breeze and a glass of California red taking the edge off. Mama Bones thinks some of her dead husband, the wild late 1960s, guns and how lucky she was to end up a grandma. Lots of water past those bridges. She hasn't fired a weapon since that night she killed the young drug addict, although she carries a Sig Sauer in her purse these days. For protection or reputation she is not certain which. Maybe a little of both. If these disagreements with the Turk get any worse, she might have to re-tune her shooting skills. She doesn't even *want* to be capo. Why can't Turk see that, huh?

Gianni joins her on the porch carrying a portable house phone. "Austin's on the line. Says Vic showed up at the restaurant on Broad Street—that Taki's."

"Vic?" Mama Bones spills her wine grabbing the phone. "Is my Vic okay?"

"Yes and no," Austin says. "He walked—"

"What do you mean, yes and no, you mamaluke? Is my Vic okay or not?"

"He's okay, but Emma Tierney is a bitch," Austin says. "Her two dogs were hustling me outside when Vic walked in and got punched. But he was holding his own when I broke free and ran out the back. Vic was giving as good as he got."

"You left him fighting?" In the silence, Mama Bones sucks in a chest full of air. It would be nice if Smarty Pants surprised her once.

"Well, yeah," Austin says. "I wanted to get free and call you."

Ha. "Who punched my Vic? How come?"

"Emma Tierney told me to wait in the bar fifteen minutes while she flirted with some pock-marked pale Russian guy. So—"

"Pock-marked, pale Russian guy?" Mama Bones repeats Austin's words out loud so Gianni can hear. He knows why she did it, too. She can tell Gianni recognizes the description.

Austin saying, "Yeah. Bald with pock marks like a moon. Skin like flour."

"Did he have an accent?" Mama Bones asks.

"Yeah. That's why I called him Russian."

"It has to be Kalinski," Gianni whispers.

Mama Bones' heart beats faster. First time since last Monday's *Days of Our Lives* recap show she's felt her pulse pick up. How does a meeting with Emma Tierney turn into a fight with Turk's man Kalinski? She set up Austin's meeting with Emma by calling Barbara Ryder. Does that mean Ryder has a connection to the Turk? Makes sense. The horse owner angle again.

"Who picked the fight at Taki's?" Mama Bones asks.

"The Russian guy hit me after I mentioned Emma's recent relationship with Heriberto. How do you know this Kalinski?"

Okay, now she understands. Mama Bones would bet a thousand dollars Austin used the words *hump* and *stable boy*. She takes the telephone away from her mouth, reaches her hand up to Gianni's arm and says, "Feel like some sushi?"

Gianni nods, helps Mama Bones rise from the wicker chair. He's such a nice boy. She can clean up the spilled wine later.

"You drive," she says. "Do we need anything from the house?"

"Nope," Gianni says. "I have weapons and ammo in my trunk."

"Okay, Smarty Pants," she says to the telephone. "Stay there on Broad Street and wait for us. Me and Gianni are on our way."

THREE

Rats. It won't take Mama Bones and Gianni two minutes to get here. There's not enough time for me to run across the street to Walgreen's and secure some medical remedy, maybe an ointment. I overheard Gianni tell Mama Bones not to worry, he had weapons and ammo in the trunk. Immediately my skin broke out in a wicked rash.

I'm lurking in the shadows, on the corner two doors down from Taki's, soon once again to risk life and limb because Mama Bones won't let me ditch her son's business. Logic and instinct say I should leave town. But I can't. Not with Luis still in jail and the plan to free him currently failing, thanks to me. I might be able to hide from an angry Mama Bones, but I can't hide from my own conscience. Luis would never leave me in jail, framed for murder.

I stick a finger inside my collar to stretch the cotton material away from my overheated neck. Our late June weather is typically hot and sticky, with the sun's disappearance each night having little or no effect on the humidity and temperature. Tonight is a perfect example. Still in the eighties, and muggy. In southern California where I grew up, the difference between night and day could be twenty degrees. I must have been crazy to move.

A white Ford panel truck bursts out of Taki's parking lot and turns toward the intersection where I lurk behind a utility pole. The unmarked van squeals through an orange light, tipping too much weight onto its right side as the truck skids into the southbound lane of Broad

Street. A street light brightens up the panel truck's cab, and I can see Full Moon driving—Kalinski, Mama Bones called him. Within ten feet of me, the truck fish tails and brushes the curb. The rear doors swing open. My partner Vic Bonacelli lies on the van's floor, a dark stain on his white toga.

The truck speeds away. No time to get my car behind Taki's. Nothing to do but watch the panel truck head south. It's nine o'clock, but the sky still holds some blue on June 29th, and the light's good. The white van travels on Broad Street in the direction of Asbury Park, but slows after two blocks and makes a left off Broad onto Reckless Place. The turn puts them near the offices of Bonacelli Investments, formerly Carr Securities, but Reckless is a numbered county road heading toward the ocean. The white truck could be going anywhere on the Jersey shore.

A blue and green NJ Transit bus blisters past the corner I stand on, it's rumbling exhaust issuing a sudden loud pop when it slows halfway down the block. Instinctively I duck. Trucks, buses, firecrackers, even champagne corks are a menace to my psyche these days—a resemblance and reminder of the barrage of gunshots I've encountered since affiliation with the Bonacellis. Forty-eight hours ago, I made up my mind to get out of my partnership with them. How did I let Mama Bones drag me back aboard her dreadful ship of war?

Oh, yeah. Luis.

A familiar black Cadillac Escalade slides up to the curb beside me. The headlights keep interior identities hidden until the passenger window rolls down with an audible squeak. Mama Bones stares at me, her hair in a scarf. Gianni's driving, his gaze straight ahead, his fingers tapping the wheel.

"Is Vic still inside that sushi joint?" Mama Bones asks.

I point south on Broad Street. "No. Kalinski has him. They went that way in a white panel truck one minute ago, made a left onto Reckless."

"You sure Vic was with him?" she asks.

"I saw Vic in the back of the van, yes."

"Vic was okay?"

"He might have been hurt, Mama Bones."

"Aye! Get in. Quick."

The SUV's rear door clicks smoothly open, then solidly shut after I climb inside. No use arguing. Vic is Mama Bones' beloved son and my partner. Vic and I have been estranged since I won control of the firm two years ago, but I'm pretty sure Mama Bones will kill me if I don't help. I'm the one who saw what I just saw. Only my eyeballs can identify that white delivery truck.

I struggle to buckle myself into the back seat, Gianni not waiting for me as he zooms a hard right onto Broad. My butt slides across the Caddy's slick leather. At least the air-conditioning feels good. A middle-aged blonde in a silver Honda SUV zooms out of a bank's drive-up window, slams on her brakes two yards short of hitting us. She honks. Gianni uses one hand to drive, the other to wave at the blonde with a middle finger. He asks, "Kalinski turned left on Reckless?"

"Yes."

"Vic was breathing?" Mama Bones asks.

"Sure." A small lie. I have no clue. "But I couldn't see that well or for very long. I recognized Vic and the toga I saw him in earlier. I saw a little blood, too, Mama Bones."

She groans.

"Who's Kalinski?" I ask.

"Turk's muscle," Mama Bones says. "You sure it was him driving the van?"

"Positive. If he works for the Turk, doesn't that mean Emma's aunt gave us up?"

"I don't think Croc Tierney's sister would spit in my face like that," Mama Bones says. "What do you think, Gianni? Did Barbara Ryder go right to the Turk after I called her?"

Gianni clicks on the Escalade's blinker before pulling up to the signal at Reckless. A blue light on the dashboard illuminates his angled features with each turn-signal click. He searches Mama Bones' face.

"It's okay to talk," she says. "Austin deserves to hear what I got him into."

"If Kalinski was there on purpose to grab Austin—and that's sure what it looks like—it means Ryder is in with Turk and the Turk is totally pissed off at us. He's not happy with the deal we offered."

"What deal?" I ask.

"I'll tell you later," Mama Bones says. "Go on, Gianni."

"It's possible Kalinski knows Emma Tierney from someplace else, or he saw her at the track and wants to try his luck. Maybe he thought he was getting someplace and totally freaked when Austin insulted her."

"No way," I say. "He tried to kidnap me. They were taking me somewhere until Vic barged in."

"Maybe you insulted her worse than you remember," Mama Bones says. "Did you say anything about humping? You like to use that word."

"Maybe," I say.

The signal changes to green. Gianni eases the Caddy forward and turns left.

"Vic is what's important," Mama Bones says. "We'll ask Kalinski why he was there when we see him."

"Is that the van?" Gianni asks. "The one parked behind Bonacelli Investments?"

Bonacelli Investments' parking lot, the building and the business—all significantly mortgaged—are actually mine, not Vic's, at least to the tune of fifty-one percent. I've agreed to sell control, but not until next year. "That's the van," I say. "Look, the back doors are still open."

Gianni nestles the SUV against the curb on Reckless. Bonacelli Investments is on our left, across the street and down half a block, the third red brick structure from the corner. I can see into my own company's parking lot through our neighbors' lots, a Chinese take-out and a defunct antique store. Gianni's thick right hand reaches under his camp shirt, sets something down on the console between himself and Mama Bones. It's a semiautomatic pistol.

"What do you want to do?" he asks Mama Bones.

"The van is parked beside the girls' trailer," she says. "Kalinski must figure he already kidnapped my son, why stop there. He's checking out the girls, seeing if they're the ones Turk lost. How'd he find out they were here?"

"Or, thanks to Ryder, this is what the Turk had in mind all night," Gianni says.

Mama Bones removes a handgun from her purse. "I say we drive in shooting."

"Let me call for back-up," Gianni says. He thumbs a cell phone.

"Wait a minute," I say.

Mama Bones cranks her face in my direction. "Get down on the floor and stay quiet. If things work out bad for me and Gianni, you call the cops, although you might feel better about yourself if you don't let Kalinski drive away with my girls. Turk bought and sold them as sex slaves. On average, they won't live five years, and compared to how they spend their time, most don't mind dying."

"My God. Where did they come from?" I ask.

She checks Gianni, who is still texting, then says, "These children are from Thailand. Sex toys for super rich Asian gamblers. Twelve years old. This is why Turk and I have been fighting for a month. I'm not gonna let my people be part of any slavery. Turk tried to deliver these four girls to Atlantic City, but we fixed it so they escaped. I'm going to help them start a new life. You in, or do you wanna run away? I give you fifteen seconds."

I nod. "I'm in."

"Okay, get down on the floor."

"Yes, ma'am." I've had enough gunplay in my life, and I'm not in the least embarrassed to slide down to the SUV's rear carpet. I'm a stockbroker, not a *pistolero*. Plus, there's more room than you'd expect in the back of an Escalade.

As I squeeze my shoulders between the back of Mama Bones' bucket seat and the bench I previously sat on, however, the worth of these girls' cause begins to nibble at my heart. My daughter Beth is several years beyond twelve, but not so long ago I've forgotten what a child she was. The baby inside. I've also read stories and heard worse tales from Jersey Troopers about the special V.I.P. rooms in Atlantic City. Exactly what goes on. Makes me ashamed to be from Jersey. Only a U.S. Federal task force can make arrests down there because three-quarters of Jersey's politicians, public and private labor unions and the police forces, not to mention the remnants of Philadelphia and New York organized crime crews—everybody gets a piece of the Atlantic City gambling take. Child sex slaves are extremely unpopular with everybody, but they remain a must for certain high rollers who account for millions in casino revenues. If the Jersey casinos won't fix these assholes up, Vegas and Singapore will.

Gianni push-buttons open the SUV's windows. Warm moist air fills the Escalade's interior. My skin grows sticky. I climb back up on the seat. "If there's going to be shooting, I could use a weapon," I say.

Mama Bones smiles. "Give him your back-up, Gianni."

From somewhere low—an ankle strap around his leg or from under the seat—Gianni produces a five-shot revolver. A Smith & Wesson. I find the correct release and check the cylinder to make sure the weapon is loaded. I lean back, the revolver aimed at the floor between my legs. I keep my forefinger on the trigger guard.

Okay, it's a big change. I know. And I don't exactly understand where this flip-flop in me comes from. Not exactly. I don't know these children Mama Bones rescued, but it's easy to imagine my daughter Beth at twelve and then cringe at the idea she could wind up in these circumstances. The other thing, I need to do something to help besides hide on the floor.

When a break opens in traffic, Gianni stabs the gas. The SUV zips across both lanes of Reckless Place into the alley behind the parking lots. The SUV's shoulder strap tugs against my neck, and the Smith & Wesson pulls on my gut. What am I doing? I reminded myself minutes ago I'm a stockbroker, not a *pistolero*, and yet here I am, rushing into battle.

I take a breath. What I'm doing is right. There are children in a trailer on my property and some bald-headed bastard wants to steal them, sell them as sex slaves. The idea makes me angry. The fact that the trailer is on my property and that I pay taxes to people who benefit from slavery in this state makes this disaster partly my responsibility.

We pass the bankrupt antique store's lot, then a two-story brick building with boarded windows across the alley. A motorcycle screeches above the other traffic on Broad Street a block away. The whine tickles my skin like an itch.

Gianni swings into the Bonacelli lot and skids to a halt behind Kalinski's white panel truck. The van's double rear doors are ajar, but not enough to see inside. There are no other cars in the lot, no sign of Kalinski or his yellow-shirted helper. The trailer with Mama Bones' girls sits on cement blocks to the right of the white van, the trailer's flimsy door wide open. Two steel steps form an entrance.

Kalinski appears in the trailer doorway, one arm encircling a young girl's tiny waist, the other arm extended toward our SUV and aiming a large pistol at the driver's side of our windshield. I gag when I look closely at the young girl Kalinski uses as a shield. She's so young. Her silk kimono shines a startling cobalt blue in the SUV's headlights.

Gianni snaps open his door and sinks to the asphalt a split second before Kalinski fires, hitting the windshield. I duck toward the driver's side of the back seat where I can see Gianni roll forward, along the side of the SUV. Kalinski fires again, the bullets opening small, spidery holes in the front glass. Another shot from Kalinski splinters Mama Bones' headrest.

Air rushes into my lungs. I didn't realize I'd been holding my breath. The exploding glass, fiery flashes and gunfire have my adrenaline surging as I drop outside the Escalade. Bullets thud against the rolled steel.

Mama Bones peeks halfway up, aims her Sig Sauer through the open passenger window like she's battling

Apaches from a stagecoach, but it's Gianni who fires twice from the front. The first shot splatters the trailer's plastic siding ten to twelve inches above Kalinski's head, but the second shot hits the top of his shoulder, six inches above the Asian child's head. A risky shot, but Gianni made it.

Kalinski falls back inside the trailer. The young girl he held as a shield scampers free down the trailer steps. Across town, a police siren blares to life.

Gianni runs to the young girl, points her toward the Escalade, then leans inside where Kalinski disappeared. Weapon ready, Gianni goes all the way in.

Mama Bones scampers to the white panel truck. I cover the trailer as she opens the rear doors and climbs inside beside Vic. Her son lies on his back. I move closer, my gun still aimed at the trailer entrance. Duct tape wraps Vic's hands and ankles.

"Vittorio?" she says. "Can you hear me?"

"Yeah," Vic says.

The sirens turn onto Broad Street.

Behind me, Gianni drags Kalinski's limp body down the trailer steps. Full Moon's face is streaked red with blood, the image startlingly bright in the SUV's headlights. At best, Kalinski is unconscious. For the first time tonight, I get a sense of what is really happening, the kind of war I am now involved in.

Yikes.

Mama Bones and I rip at the duct tape binding Vic. He groans, and when his hands are free, he checks himself where blood smears his bed-sheet toga. The wound, a cut on his lower torso, appears superficial, the bleeding already stopped.

"Should I bring Kalinski?" Gianni asks. "We could get rid of him later."

Mama Bones shakes her head. "Leave him for the

cops. Get the girls in the Escalade and take them to my house. They should be safe there for now. Maybe call some extra men to come over."

Gianni drops Kalinski like dirty underwear. The bald man's pock-mocked head bounces off our parking lot's black asphalt. At the trailer entrance, three young Asian girls are eager to join their friend in escape. They're already packed and dressed for travel—jeans and T-shirts. All three rush past Gianni toward the SUV. Two girls tow carry-on airline suitcases.

We get Vic stretched out in the back and take off. The packed SUV—there's me, Gianni, Mama Bones, Vic and four young Asian ladies—reach Reckless Place before a Branchtown Police car rounds the corner from Broad Street. He drives right past us. The blinking blue and red lights play Halloween shadow tricks with the thick-leafed trees and parking meter poles.

"Did the deal you made with the Turk involve our mutually owned investment company?" I ask.

"Forget about it," Mama Bones says. "I'll tell you later. I'm busy with my boy now, huh?"

"Drop me off at Taki's then," I say. "I need my car. All I want to know is if—"

"Call to me tonight, okay? I'm gonna wait for your call."

FOUR

Mama Bones, Gianni, Vic and the rescued girls drop me a minute later at Taki's curb. Walking toward the back parking lot, I check my cell phone for messages. Nothing urgent. My two kids Beth and Ryan are on a trip with the ex-wife and her boyfriend, the dentist.

I exchange my phone for the car keys in my pocket, although the car's probably unlocked. When I arrived earlier tonight to meet what's her face—Emma Tierney—I didn't expect to be inside Taki's more than twenty minutes.

Even in a nearly full lot, my low-slung Solara is easy to spot, the moon glaring off its light brown ragtop and the severely slanted windshield. I hurry, my imagination working on a hot shower and bed, which is yet another reason I am totally unsuited to further association with Mama Bones and her son Vic: my body is exhausted from these minor heroic activities. Adrenaline plays havoc with my muscles, mental acuity and general sense of well-being. I can't imagine why thrill-seekers chase the stuff.

The Toyota's interior lights up as I yank open the driver's door, and I stifle a yelp. I can't prevent another pump of adrenaline, however. What was a shadow in the passenger seat is now a human: Emma Tierney.

"I need to talk to you," she says.

My heart's pounding, but I hesitate only a second before dropping inside next to the redhead. Thus my self-inflicted warning—Austin, you are completely irrational about redheaded women, you should be running, not sitting down—comes way too late. I'm already within her sphere of influence; i.e., I can breathe, smell and taste her. I imagine the freckles I can't see.

The problem could go back to *I Love Lucy* reruns. Sexy women who make you laugh are damn hard to beat in the lover department, and redheaded Lucille Ball reminds me of that perfect combo every time I see one of her old TV shows. However, this harmful if not uncommon male quirk has earned me four decades of embarrassment, black eyes, broken hearts and physical misfortune to go along with whatever fun-filled sex I enjoyed on the way. Thus, as I sit beside the same woman who only an hour ago flirted with that kidnapper Kalinski, I should worry, not work on my charm. Is it possible that, once again, I'm letting this obsession for redheads cloud my judgment?

Oh well, who cares. Crazy has always been the word that best fits my behavior around redheaded women. In twelve-step programs like Alcoholics and Narcotics Anonymous, members and literature define insanity as repeating the same behavior over and over expecting different results. I'm pretty sure the idea of humans repeating their mistakes time and time again precedes twelve-step programs. Probably goes back to the first Greek playwrights. But I'm sure of one thing: addictive behavior comes in all shapes, sizes and colors, and my actions clearly meet the first criteria of addiction. Is this redheaded obsession causing trouble in your life? Like booze, heroin and meth? Of course it's causing trouble. I'm risking my life by even talking to this woman again.

At least I know why. I mean, the woman looks great. Emma Tierney's wine-red hair catches light from the moon through my windshield, and that canopy of freckles glows above the neckline of her silk blouse. Love her three-inch hoop earrings. She smiles sexy and clean, like a toothpaste commercial, and inside me, a semi-rusty burner fires up. I haven't encountered more than a passing sexual stimulation since Patricia Willis left for Boston last year. That's strange for me. Until Patricia, I typically fell in love once a month. Even stranger, only hours ago this Emma person suggested I might be deaf or stupid.

"What do you want to talk about?" I ask.

"I wanted to explain why I was so rude."

Her low-pitched voice hums on my skin like a purring cat. Her glistening eyes flirt with promise in the dark front seat. But on keen observation, I detect a vague ennui or emptiness lurking inside her. I can't say for sure. But my gut feels Emma might be more than a little odd.

Oh boy. I love oddballs. "I know why you were mean to me earlier tonight," I say. "That bald Russian guy had a gun on you."

Emma laughs, the low pitch of her voice tickling my thighs. Oh my. Or is that tingling sensation the result of something else...like someone standing outside my car window, directly behind my head?

Emma gasps and cold metal touches the back of my neck. A glimpse of a yellow torso flashes in the mirror, and a man's voice whispers, "My gun's even bigger. Get out of the car."

Mama Bones fires the stove's main burner. Ten o'clock is a funny time to be doing all this cooking, but Vic said he was hungry after his kidnapping, Gianni and Tomas, too. And as long as she's at the stove, Mama Bones might as well cook some of these early tomatoes for freezing. She watches the water in the stainless steel pot rise steadily to a rolling boil. Her nephews Gianni and Tomas are waiting at the table beside Vic, three hungry men, all of them ready to eat a dish of late-night Bolognese.

Almost ready. Mama Bones is happy to cook, pleased her son Vic is here with his mama and well enough to be hungry. The wound on his stomach is a scratch from a belt buckle or something. Makes her feel like Christmas, Vic being at the house and talking again.

She slips two pounds of imported fettuccine into the water and stirs with a wooden spoon to separate the long strands of pasta. The stove top is crowded, and a couple of blue flames go orange when hot water splashes near the burners. Besides water for the pasta, she has two, ten-gallon pots of home grown tomatoes simmering—most to be frozen—and a twelve-inch fry pan crisping up half a dozen *zeppole*. Some people think it's strange to have two kitchens, but not older Italians. The kitchen upstairs, you keep all nice and clean. Show your pretty bowls and knickknacks. Down in the basement kitchen, you keep a dirt floor, handle the messy stuff. When she was a kid, many parents of Mama Bones' friends kept and butchered chickens in the dirt basement. Used the chicken poop to produce extra-tasty vegetables in the yard.

It's nice and quiet down here. Cozy, too. At the little round table, Vic and her nephews drink wine, nibble on mozzarella and roasted red peppers, a sight that reminds her to sip from her own glass. The radio is on softly, Motown sounds from her high school days tickling her feet to dance. The Bolognese sauce smells good.

The world would be a good place tonight if it wasn't for Johnny The Turk Korsay.

"So what you think, Gianni," Mama Bones says. "The Turk's men say he's up to something. Are we in a war?"

"Starting to look like it," he says.

Mama Bones wonders if maybe she made a mistake not finishing off Kalinski. Why should she worry about him showing up somewhere now, maybe hurting Vic or her nephews? "Should we ask for a meeting?"

"I'd let it go another day or so," Gianni says, "see if he makes a move."

Tomas coughs, wants to talk. Good. He never says nothing.

"If it's going to be war, why wait?" Tomas says. "We should hit Turk first. First and hard."

Mama Bones knows such violent strategies only make sense in books and movies. Tomas next is going to say it's time to hit the mattresses. Ha. No one in her crew or probably the Turk's crew was ever in a war. And nobody wants one either. That happens, everybody's out of business. The Turk is the boss. He still has to act tough. But the majority of his lieutenants—the big earners like Mama Bones—are mostly business men and women, shop keepers and club owners, plumbers and electricians.

"Tomas watches too much TV," Gianni says. "Kalinski went too far grabbing Vic, either on his own or on orders from Turk. But you shot him for his trouble. And the girls are safe. Let's wait, see what Turk does."

Mama Bones adjusts the flame on the boiling water. "Turk always goes too far. That's how he got to be boss—the way he was since we were kids. Beating up everybody who called him Fat Johnny."

"Fat Johnny?"

"Yeah, in those days," Mama Bones says, "Turk was as round as a bowling ball."

* * *

Mama Bones waits until after dinner, until Vic falls asleep upstairs watching television and Tomas goes outside on the patio to smoke his fancy Cuban cigar. Just her and Gianni downstairs in the dirt kitchen. She refills Gianni's cup from a metal, flip-over espresso maker Vic gave her a few Christmases ago.

"Your Bolognese sauce is the world standard," Gianni says.

Mama Bones returns to the kitchen sink and grabs a dirty pot. The sink came from a second-hand restaurant supply store, holds enough water to bathe two German Sheppards at the same time. She snaps on the hot water faucet. Her feet are ready for bed. Heavy as lead weights.

"Leave the dishes," Gianni says. "Tomas and I'll do them later."

"I got it," she says. "Two pots, a couple of plates in the dish washer. I want you to think about something before you answer. Okay?" She stares across the space into Gianni's eyes, those long pretty lashes. "I heard a story the Turk is planning something big at the racetrack this weekend. Probably Sunday. What I need to know, do you think he could rob the racetrack's cash-counting room?"

Gianni shakes his head. "Impossible. Even with twenty armed men. It's at the center of a maze of sealed hallways, gates and doors. Electronic security is everywhere. You can't get *in*, let alone get *out* with the cash."

"But," Mama Bones says, "I hear he's been planning seven or eight years, maybe more. And he's got inside help."

Gianni stands and takes his cup and saucer to the sink. So light on his feet, this boy. A great dancer. He rinses his cup. "Even if he could do it, which he can't, robbing the state-owned racetrack would bring more new badges around here than a Presidential motorcade. Everybody's operations would be threatened. Turk wouldn't do anything so stupid."

Mama Bones sips her espresso. "Okay. Go to bed, get a good night's sleep. When you wake up tomorrow, all fresh and smart, you gotta figure out what the Turk is up to, because I'm telling you, he's making big plans."

Mama Bones grips the dirty sauce pot with strong forearms and tender hands, like she was holding a brand new baby. The idea makes her smile. She wonders if in her lifetime she's bathed more giant pots or children in this sink. She smiles, thinking of Vic, and then shrugs. What the heck is she going to do with him?

"All right," Gianni says. "I'm going to bed and turn on the Yankees. They're in Los Angeles tonight."

Mama Bones finishes washing, stuffs the sauce pot in a cupboard underneath the counter. Austin Carr the stockbroker grew up in Los Angeles. Wasn't he supposed to call her tonight? She wipes the kitchen counter, pours herself a third glass of wine and picks up her phone.

I wondered what happened to the man in the yellow golf shirt, why he wasn't in the van with Kalinski. Now I know: turns out he and the redhead waited for me at Taki's, and now I've been captured again.

Thirty minutes after climbing inside my Toyota beside Emma Tierney, I'm horizontal, not vertical or sitting, my hands and arms pinned to my side. Cinched straps cross my chest and thighs, pressing me tight against a modified stretcher. I'm only slightly confused how the yellow-shirted man packed me in the rear of this ambulance so quickly, although bewilderment and confusion seem to be basic elements of my nature.

A guy knows in his heart when he's a screw-up.

I remember Emma in my passenger seat, followed quickly by Yellow Shirt, the gun, Yellow Shirt's new unseen friend, the beating, being hauled into the backseat of a car, driven someplace and finally strapped onto this stretcher in a red and white private ambulance. I smell fish. And there are boats all around. I don't think these fellows brought me to a hospital.

I am so screwed. I can't believe this is all happening again—Austin Carr, stockbroker, forced into improbable and dangerous battles with armed wrongdoers, in this case, people I bet are employed by the Turk.

If I had a working brain, I never would have returned from the vacation Mama Bones sent me on to reconsider my earlier resignation. In fact, looking back on the list of spectacularly unfortunate events since that time, I should have changed my name and run away to Puerto Vallarta the day after I saw Heriberto killed. That's what this harassment is all about: I saw the Turk with Heriberto. I saw Turk's men. I saw the racehorse's back hooves when that gray filly tried to kill me, and in that out-of-the-way stable office, I saw Turk shoot Heriberto in the head. Murder. Of course I have a bulls eye on my back. From the Turk's point of view, Austin Carr is a deadly, poison-tipped loose end.

"Leave him on the stretcher, even when we put him on the boat," Yellow Shirt says. "I got a fun idea."

Boat? Fun idea? The ambulance's side-hinged rear door snaps open behind my head, and cool and damp salt air gushes inside. My stomach flips. I have what you might call a poor history with boats and the ocean. Apparently it's turned into a full-course phobia.

My stretcher plummets from the back of the ambulance, the two wheels below my head crashing onto the hard surface of a dockside parking lot. The steel contraption clatters like pots and pans. My head rattles like dishes.

"Push him out onto the dock," Yellow Shirt says. "That stretcher rolls good."

Half an hour later, the three of us battle wind and waves as we sail the open sea. Actually, we're in Raritan Bay, not the open sea, but it feels like the Gulf of Alaska out here late at night, the choppy water bouncing us around in a stiff breeze. Maybe it's just me. I'm also convinced the buzzing on my thigh must be a stun gun. I know Yellow Shirt and his friend are going to torture me. Any second this strange ticklish vibration will transform into spine-twisting agony. I will be forced to scream like a five-year-old, my lonely voice a whisper, lost inside the wind.

Oh, get over yourself, Carr.

A wave bigger than most lifts the bow of this multi-million-dollar motor yacht, launching my rolling stretcher along the deck toward the stern. Somebody greased up the wheels of this mobile bed, too. Not a stutter or a squeak. Zipping along rather quickly. Luckily, I'm not a prisoner aboard the Queen Mary where I'd have a few hundred feet to gather momentum. Though my cart and I crash solidly into the stern railing, we don't have enough speed to fly over the top.

Not yet anyway. Maybe next time.

My traveling stretcher knocks gently against the stern guard rail a few times, then we're off again, rolling forward toward the bow. Laughter from inside the wheelhouse grinds my teeth as the Austin Carr Express sails by. Those bastards. Captain Yellow Shirt and his mate. I can't see their faces well behind the windscreen glass, but I can tell both of them are watching and enjoying themselves. They're waving.

The night sky is black with rain clouds, but we're close enough to Sandy Hook that I can make out the peninsula's flat outline on my right. The starboard side, I think. Lights blink at me from the U.S. Coast Guard dock near the very tip of the national park. I lift my face to see what's ahead. A spray of salt water moistens my face, but above the bow I make out a tiny string of lights that is the Verrazano Bridge. We can't be that far from New York Harbor and the open Atlantic Ocean. The sea will be much rougher. I'm going to end up in the water, strapped forever to this steel stretcher, rotting in the muck at the bottom of the sea.

For now, however, the waves balance me. The stretcher comes to a halt near the boat's center, and I feel that buzzing tickle again on my thigh. Wait a minute. That's not some torture. The stretcher, the straps, the sea and my imagination are the torture. The buzzing tickle is my cell phone set on silent ring. Perfect timing. Probably the ex-wife Susan asking if my will's been updated.

It's takes some major wiggling, my arms being cinched to my sides, but I touch the phone through my slacks with one fingertip. On my model, I can do a lot with one fingertip. I answer and set the phone on external speaker, plus raise the volume to maximum.

"Hello?" I shout because the boat deck is noisy, to say the least.

"Hey, Smarty Pants," Mama Bones says. "I thought you were going to call me. Where are you? That's a lot of wind."

Though muffled by the material of my pants, Mama Bones' familiar cackle still cuts through the air like thunder. Considering she got me into this mess, not to mention all the past endangerments she's tossed my way,

I'm surprised how the sound of her voice gives me hope.

"Help, Mama Bones. I'm captured again." Though my brain makes sense of it all, my mouth feels a little strange talking to my leg.

Yellow Shirt scrambles from the wheelhouse. His giant mitts grab the stretcher while he stares at my pants, the material stretched tightly over my thigh where the phone glows. A rectangle of lime green light reflects onto Yellow Shirt's square face.

"What's the matter, huh?" Mama Bones says.

Yellow Shirt says, "Mama Bones?"

My mind blinks, or shorts, or something. I don't understand. He's repeating her name because...

"I heard that voice before," Mama Bones says. "Who is this?"

"Hey, Mama Bones. It's Billy Z."

"Billy Zantori from Bayonne? Camille the Lady Butcher's boy?"

"That's me," Yellow Shirt says. "I can't believe I'm talking to Mama Bones Bonacelli in the middle of Raritan Bay. How do you know this mope stockbroker?"

Bouncing off satellites, probably crossing signals and blowing fuses across wireless networks nationwide, Mama Bones issues a sizzling screech: "Bayyyooooone Billy."

FIVE

Considering all that's happened lately, a phone call from Mama Bones during a stretcher-trapped sea cruise isn't *that* strange. There's not enough space or time to run through everything on my bizarro list of recent victimizations, but for example, during the last four years I've been yanked over the side of boat by a bluefin tuna, chased through the Jersey Pine Barrens by a monster called the Creeper and conned into romance by a magic love potion. Watching a yellow shirted hit man—Bayonne Billy—converse with a green light on my leg really doesn't rank far above normal.

"I'm getting ready to dump this turkey in New York Harbor," Billy says.

"The Turk told you to kill him?" Mama Bones asks.

"Yeah, and have fun first if I want. You ever eat those sausages Mom sent youse for Christmas?"

"What?"

"Ha ha ha. I'm only kidding, Mama Bones."

"Oh Mother Mary."

"Ha ha ha."

Mama Bones coughs. "Listen, Billy, we got a problem. That guy you're about to drown is Austin Carr, a very famous stockbroker. My son's partner." Above the gusting wind, Mama Bones' voice crackles even louder. "Somebody probably forgot to mention that to the Turk."

"Yeah," Billy says. "Probably."

I must say I'm pleased with Mama Bones' description of my fame, no matter how ridiculous it sounds. Third-party endorsements are so powerful. Also, I appreciate the urgency of her tone as she haggles for my life. At the very least, her praise alleviates the self-loathing produced by my decision to climb into a car with Emma Tierney.

What a dope!

Mama Bones' buzz-saw voice again rattles my thigh. "You watch-a your mouth, Billy Zantori. I don't like sarcastic. You think I'm telling you some kind of lies?"

"This guy is really your son's business partner?"

"You got a smart phone, check him out on Google."

"Look, Mama Bones. Who he is don't matter. I have to do what the Turk tells me—take this mope out to deep water and dump him—or I'll be the one disappears next. You *know* this is a true story."

"No, you can't do that, Billy. You gotta bring Austin back to the shore. I'll come pick him up myself. Where you gonna dock, huh? Atlantic Highlands?"

"You know I can't go against the Turk."

"I'll talk to him," Mama Bones says. "We've been friends since high school."

"I can't."

"Billy, you have to."

"I got a job to do for the Turk, Mama Bones. You're interfering. I'm sorry, but—"

"Hey," Mama Bones says. "Maybe you think I can't send you back to Bayonne as a box of meatloaf patties, huh?"

"Jesus, Mama Bones. What am I gonna do? The Turk will kill me."

"You hurt that stockbroker, I'm gonna kill you, Billy Zantori from Bayonne. Only first, I'm gonna chop up your mama Camille, make you watch. I'm sending Gianni up to Bayonne right now to grab her unless you turn that boat around."

"Jesus."

* * *

Back at Billy Z's mooring spot in the Atlantic Highlands municipal marina twenty minutes later, Tomas and Gianni come aboard to get me. Mama Bones stands behind them sipping a large coffee from Dunkin Donuts. Must be after midnight when I'm released and escorted into the parking by Tomas. Mama Bones and Gianni linger on the dock to discuss my future with Billy Zantori.

At the familiar black Escalade in a near-empty parking lot, the air still hot and muggy despite the hour, Tomas stuffs me in the back seat, then leans against the big Caddy to light a cigarette. He enjoys his tobacco, too, drawing deeply and exhaling through carefully pursed lips. I used to think he and Gianni were twins, both of them dark skinned with stocky, six-foot frames, major Roman noses. But all of Tomas' parts are a little smaller and a little quicker I notice now, especially his smile when he catches me watching him smoke.

Mama Bones shakes her head violently as she, Gianni and Billy stroll toward the Escalade. Walking slowly. Lots of arm waving and hand gestures; locked in semi-heated exchange, all offering frank and dramatic facts no doubt to bolster their respective arguments. Billy does not look happy, and he is definitely not scoring points with his point of view. Wish I could hear what he's saying.

I'm confused why Mama Bones is fighting so hard for my survival. I must mean more to the Bonacellis than a caretaker for their stock and bond business. It's as if the old gal has big plans for me.

I try the window button. The glass slides down. The sound of water slapping against a nearby yacht filters inside the Caddy, as does the whine of a generator.

Billy's voice rises above everything else: "The Turk will find him."

Tomas turns to me and stares. His eyes narrow, then he waves his glowing cigarette in a circular motion. He wants me to roll up the window.

It takes five or six more minutes of negotiation, Billy and Mama Bones standing eighteen inches apart. But Billy Z finally nods his head.

She hugs him.

Gianni hands him a thickly packed, letter-size envelope.

Sure we have leaders in this state—mayors, a governor, district representatives, senators and councilmen. And our multi-million-dollar horse estates in the northwest harbor European crown princes and a British knight or two. But in Jersey, cash is the only king.

Gianni opens the Escalade's passenger door for her, suggesting Mama Bones ride in the shotgun seat while he drives. But Mama Bones chooses to climb in the back with Austin, the smarty pants stockbroker badly in need of a trip to the 'splaining department.

How come these people don't understand what kind of world they live in, huh? Bayonne Billy, Austin Carr, her own son Vic. It's not about right and wrong. It's about unbending, pigheaded will.

Mama Bones stares at Austin, her bones and muscles aching. Her bedtime was four hours ago. Mother Mary is she gonna be tired tomorrow. "So Smarty Pants, Billy says the redhead Emma Tierney bagged you two times in one night. What were you thinking, huh? It's a good thing I checked on you."

Austin gives her an exaggerated nod. Grateful. "Yes, ma'am. Thank you."

Gianni starts the engine. He's grinning when he turns to back up.

"Thank you?" she says. She frowns at the poor man. Austin must have been scared out of his wits, rolling around on that stretcher, almost dropping into Raritan Bay. "Austin Carr is such a mamaluke, he sits next to the same spider that already bit him? That is dumber than dumb. You should be drowned. Some in your situation would say, I owe you my life, Mama Bones. I belong to you forever."

Austin grins like Gianni did. Everybody sure is happy.

"I think I already belong to you," Austin says. "Besides, you know I'd do the same for you."

"You would?"

"Sure I would. Absolutely."

"But you didn't. Not tonight. I save *you*, huh?"

"Yup."

"You owe me big time."

Austin nods again. "Yes I do."

He's gonna get stiff in the neck if he don't watch it, all this nodding and bowing. Not that it isn't fun to watch. Cost Mama Bones some big bucks to free Austin from Billy Z, she might as well enjoy it. "Okay then, Smarty Pants. Here's the deal. You gonna do exactly what I say. No arguments. You gonna hide out a few days from the Turk, maybe a week. Until things calm down, you're the new assistant cook at the Pardon Me Diner. You'll sleep there, too. Or at my house."

Austin gets a look on his face, goofy but not exactly happy, like Mama Bones' assistant cook idea is no good. Too bad. As of this morning, the Pardon Me's kitchen staff is short-handed.

* * *

Two days later Mama Bones watches Johnny the Turk Korsay stride across the Pardon Me's main dining room, the king-size man seventy this year, same as Mama Bones, and still swinging his big you-know-what when he walks. Proud of himself. Not brainy and quick like Austin, but street wise and tough, maybe a genius for odds and numbers. They say Turk also has a built-in, natural lie-detector.

Makes sense to Mama Bones. Before he brought the Korsay family to America in 1970, they say Turk's father was a Lebanese-born camel trader from Egypt. Made a fortune selling two-humped middle-eastern camels to Abdel Nasser's Egyptian army. You can't make up a story like that.

Mama Bones sits at her three-quarter-circle control station, the Pardon Me's biggest corner booth. She's perched near the center, at the top of the circle, the orange leather cushions stretching out from her on either side. Enough room for six or seven adults. A right-angle corner of brick walls protects her back. Over on her right side, like always, is Gianni, and behind him the four-inch thick, bulletproof bay window she had made special. On her left is nobody.

The Turk marches to the edge of her table but keeps his gaze off Mama Bones. He stands with his hands hidden inside his suit coat pockets, staring at Gianni. There's a story about him killing a rival once this way, whipping a pistol from his coat and shooting. But Mama Bones isn't worried. Too many witnesses at the Pardon Me Diner.

Turk says, "Just the two of us, Angelina."

Mama Bones glances at Gianni. He scoots around and out of the booth without a word to either one of them. She knows he won't go far, and she also knows he has two of his men in the room eating breakfast.

"Sit down and talk to me, Johnny," Mama Bones says. She almost calls him Fat Johnny, the nickname Mama Bones gave him in high school. "How come you want to see me today, huh?"

The Turk slides his six-five, two-hundred-and-sixty-pound body onto the far edge of Mama Bones' booth. Nice suit he's wearing. Charcoal gray and—what she hears—hand made in London. Over fifty thousand bucks apiece.

"Billy Z tells me you interfered with the stockbroker," Turk says.

Mama Bones' espresso is cold but not like the Turk's dark brown eyes. Frozen solid. She gives him ice cubes back, says, "I know a guy says you tried to kidnap my nieces from a trailer."

The Turk stares. She stares. A stand-off until Mama Bones thinks it's time to let him win. "What you say about the stockbroker is true. Austin's a friend and my son's business partner. I happened to call him right in the middle of...whatever Billy was doing."

"You asked Billy not to kill him and keep that a secret from me?"

Mama Bones shakes her head. The Turk's a non-Italian, but as the late capo Bluefish's accountant and chief bookmaker, Turk was earning the New York bosses tons of money for years. "Who told you that, huh?" she asks. "Not Billy because it's not true. I never said for Billy to keep a secret from you."

Marlene the waitress comes to the table with Mama Bones' special espresso pot and a clean empty cup for Turk. Mama Bones keeps her gaze on the mean nasty son of a camel trader. When Bluefish got killed, the Turk won Bluefish's capo job, supposedly a temporary thing. But the Turk earns everybody so much money, New York isn't bothering to replace him.

Mama Bones says, "You want some coffee, Johnny?"

"No thanks. Even decaf upsets my stomach."

What also helps him stay capo, Turk murdered two Italian candidates for his position. He became a problem for Mama Bones when the Turk decided to supply female children to sex monsters in Atlantic City. Until Kalinski broke into her trailer at Bonacelli Investments, she was certain she'd kept the rescue a secret.

"How about some milk and apple pie?" Mama Bones says.

Turk shakes his head and Marlene the waitress takes off, leaving the espresso and the cup in case Turk changes his mind. Without taking her eyes off him, Mama Bones pulls her cup and saucer close, pours herself a refill.

"That's the truth, Johnny. I swear on Our Mother Mary. I never said to keep a secret from you."

The Turk keeps staring at her. He's a familiar face but a very cold man, this Egyptian-born gambler. Took a lot of teenagers' money with dice and cards when they were high school kids. Beat a few up, too.

"This weekend, I have a nice play coming," Turk says. "A lot of profit, and your pal the stockbroker saw something that could screw it up. I can't afford to take any chances. New York's invested a lot in this play, too, Angelina. I'm risking more than men and money. I could be risking my life if things go bad."

Mama Bones carefully places her espresso cup in its saucer. "What happened, Johnny, I asked Billy if there was a way to keep Austin alive. That's all. When Billy said he had to kill Austin, or answer to you, I backed off. That's what happened, right? Austin Carr is dead?"

"Billy said he threw him overboard."

Mama Bones nods, adding what she hopes is a convincing smile. Turk's dark brown gaze hasn't left her face since he sat at her table. He thinks he's making her nervous, but getting stared at by the Turk is no problem for Mama Bones.

"But Billy was lying," Turk says.

Mama Bones reaches for her espresso. Uh, oh. "You sure? Billy didn't say the truth?"

"He was lying about carrying out his instructions—throwing the stockbroker overboard. He told me later, when he changed his story, that he shot and buried Carr. He stuck to that second story until he died."

Mama Bones' heart beats a little a faster. She glances at the black espresso in her cup, then back up at Turk's steady gaze. "So maybe Billy was lying when he told you he shot Carr, too, huh?"

"I couldn't judge by then," Turk says. "He stuck to the first lie too long and was in too bad a shape."

Mama Bones sniffs the rich aroma of dark roasted coffee beans. She concentrates on how much she loves her thick Italian espresso. "So you're here because you think maybe I made a deal with Billy? You think maybe Austin Carr is still alive?"

The Turk's shoulders slide up an inch, then ease back down. Smooth, like they ride on automobile shock absorbers. The man can do the Watusi, too. She remembers that well enough. Friday night dances after the high school basketball games. Sock hops, they called them back then.

"I can't tell you how big this deal is Sunday," Turk says. "I can't be worried you're working against me, that maybe you're keeping someone alive who could ruin it."

Mama Bones finishes her espresso like a shot of tequila, then studies the pattern in the leftovers. This batch of wet coffee grounds looks like a sky full of black storm clouds.

"Look up, Angelina. Look me in the eyes and tell me you're not hiding this stockbroker."

When she raises her gaze, Mama Bones wears her best poker face. Think fast but show him nothing. Blank. "Okay, Johnny, I tell you the truth. But don't get mad, huh?"

SIX

In his fancy London-made charcoal gray suit, Johnny the Turk Korsay studies his old high school rival, Mama Bones. Just like half a century ago, his dark eyes don't blink or show her what he's thinking. Turk watches her in a cool and easy way, his baseball-glove size hands resting on the coffee shop table, fingers folded together, lips grim, waiting for Mama Bones to explain what happened with Billy and Austin Carr. Turk always knew the golden rule of getting wise: you learn nothing while you talk.

Fat chance I tell you the truth, Fat Johnny. "I paid Billy twenty-five thousand to shoot the stockbroker," Mama Bones says. "I paid for Billy to shoot and bury him somewhere so I can dig him up later."

Turk's jaw sets like quick-dry cement. His eyebrows push so low, they cover half his eyeballs. "You paid Billy to disobey my orders, tried to turn him against me?"

Mama Bones sets down her espresso cup hastily. The China rattles. "No. That's not right. I offered to pay Billy twenty-five grand to shoot and bury the stockbroker instead of throwing him in the water. I figured dead is dead, what's the difference?"

"Why would you do that?"

Mama Bones spreads her hands in front of her chest like she's gonna catch a giant beach ball. "Just business, Johnny. My son Vic and I have to prove Austin Carr is one hundred percent, completely dead to the insurance company. Without a body, we can't get legal control of Bonacelli Investments for years."

Turk sighs. "So you can show me Austin Carr's body?"

"No. Billy didn't get a chance to tell me where he put him."

The Turk frowns. Uncertain.

Mama Bones tries to look like she lost a big bet. "It's a big problem. You have any idea where Billy might have stashed him? Without a body, our lawyers say it could be seven years before he's declared legally dead."

She stares confidently into Turk's probing gaze. He's pissed she did something behind his back, but he's confused about the rest. She fooled him, pretty much. Her story makes sense and he can't really believe she'd lie to him—total baloney like a cheating husband. He couldn't imagine Austin is standing fifty feet away in a fake wig and beard, the new cook, that tall skinny biker guy tossing burgers.

She pours herself more coffee from the pot Marlene left. Takes her time. Smiling at him. "Sure you don't wanna piece of pie?"

Cooking all day wears me out, and Mama Bones' den contains a soft bed, but it's a curious noise that wakes me one night only days after starting my new job. Was it voices? It's so late at night. I'm stretched horizontal on the pullout sofa-bed inside Mama Bones' screened-in back porch. The thirty-by-fifteen foot rectangular room owns a roof but only two solid walls, and warm gusts of summer wind push through the fine steel mesh to cool my sweaty neck. I must have been dreaming about sex.

That's right, I remember. Emma Tierney. Heaven help me. Those darn freckles. Strange that I'm subconsciously feeling erotic about a woman who keeps trying to get me killed. Of course she is a redhead, and so—naturally—that explains everything.

Fool.

Talking heads from the financial news desk glow on a flat-screen TV. I turned off the sound before dozing, but my makeshift bedroom blinks with brightly colored images. I'm looking for the remote when a puff of wind carries the clear, back and forth sound of a man and woman talking. Snippets of words reach me, but no meaning. They're in front. The male voice might be Gianni's.

I roll off the bed and tip toe to the screen wall. The woman raises her voice, and then mentions my name. *Austin's here, isn't he?* I recognize Emma Tierney now, and my heart rate jumps. Is that why I dreamed about her? I pinch myself. I'm awake. It's real. I can still hear her—Emma Tierney talking to Gianni on the porch or front lawn of Mama Bones' house. No one is supposed to know I'm here. I'm supposed to be dead, a missing person, a victim of Turk's justice.

Alone in the dark, searching my way through a strange house toward the front porch, it occurs to me I'm headed the wrong way.

Why am I walking *toward* the redhead?

Where the hallway meets the living room, I hear Gianni and Emma clearly, so I stop and listen. They're on the porch, the oak front door wide open. Pulse racing, I step into the parlor where their silhouettes show like an old black and white movie through Mama Bones' sheer white drapes.

"I know he's here," Emma says.

"No he's not, and I'm done talking," Gianni says. "What I heard, he disappeared and you were the last one to see him."

"I know he's here," she says.

Gianni closes the door halfway. "I'm going back to bed."

"I have to see him," Emma says. "Austin thinks I set him up—twice—but I have to tell him it's not true. I had no idea what was going to happen. I was...used."

"Go home," Gianni says.

"No, please. Ask him if he'll talk to me."

"He's not here. And if he was, I wouldn't tell you. Now get the hell out of here."

"Please."

Gianni slams and bolts the door. I duck back into the darkness and skitter down Mama Bones' hallway like a rat. I hope Emma lingers on the steps. I need thirty, forty seconds to slip my clothes on, sneak out and catch her. I know. I know. But the thing is, I believe her. She *was* used. I could hear the truth in her voice. Why would she come here at four o'clock in the morning, looking for me, if she weren't telling the truth? Just to set me up again? Report my whereabouts to the Turk?

It cannot be true.

When I'm back in my blue jeans, loafers and dress shirt, I hurry outside through the back screen porch and down the narrow side yard between Mama Bones' two-story Victorian and her neighbor's mossy Tudor. Lilies and astilbes bloom in a shade garden between the homes, the colored blossoms washed pale by the moonlight.

Emma slides into an old square Mercedes as I reach the street. I jog across the damp lawn and hit the asphalt. The excitement that propelled my heart rate higher reaches my feet. I'm not running, I'm dancing—almost flying—toward a woman who is nothing but Danger. With a capital D. I must be stark raving mad.

Five yards from the open driver's window, her engine starts. I call her name as Emma snaps on the headlights.

Her loud gasp is not for me.

In the street, fifteen yards ahead of the Mercedes, stands Mama Bones, the widow Bonacelli presented squarely in Emma's bright beams. Visible against Mama Bones' flannel nightgown is her fifteen-shot, Sig Sauer pistol.

Mama Bones raises the semiautomatic, aiming at Emma behind the windshield. "Out of the car, Jezebel."

Mama Bones still holds the weapon in her lap ten minutes later. I don't think she's going to shoot me or Emma, but being forced to sit here in Mama Bones' living room with its murky, Italian portraits—probably Grandma and Grandpa Rossi—is not encouraging.

"Stop your wise cracks and listen," Mama Bones says. "It's real simple. If the Turk finds out you're alive, he's gonna kill *every*body—Austin Carr, Mama Bones, Gianni, Tomas, all our friends, family, neighbors and pets. You understand, huh?"

I'm speechless. So is Emma. And not only because we're scared of Mama Bones and the Turk. Something else is talking to us, a special warmth radiating from the redhead's hip and thigh, burning me through her blue jeans. The plastic couch-cover facilitates a natural slide in each other's direction, and our contact is glowing hot.

"Bottom line," Mama Bones says. "Neither of you leaves this house for a while."

I nod. Fine with me. I'm hiding here anyway.

"I can't stay," Emma says. "I have walk-throughs, training sessions, appointments. I have to work."

Mama Bones waves her semiautomatic. "Mr. Sig Sauer says you're sticking around here."

"Ha." Emma's laugh sounds like a bark. Her body vibrates. "So, you'll shoot me if I try to leave?"

"Shoot you, cut you in little bitsy pieces and feed you to the Navasquan River crabs," Mama Bones says.

Emma shakes her head. "Here's the thing, Mrs. Bonacelli. Even if I stay, I'll probably get shot. Aren't you curious how I knew Austin was here?"

"You didn't know, you guessed," Mama Bones says. "You figured if Austin was still alive, who could protect him better than me, huh? You got lucky. You're probably here to check things out for the Turk. That's what you've been doing all the time, huh?"

Emma likes to shake her noggin. It makes those long wine-red curls dance on the edge of her shoulders. "My father told me Austin was here. He says there's going to be trouble."

Mama Bones' eyes narrow. Gianni straightens up. Emma's father is Branchtown's ex-mayor, Stephen "Crocodile" Tierney, the guy who skipped bail after a Federal indictment. Quit paying his mortgage on the Pardon Me Diner. Loves the horses.

"How would your father know?" Mama Bones asks. "*Time* magazine says he's probably in Argentina. Maybe the Philippines."

"My father's in Branchtown, staying with the Turk. They're friends. Turk is helping my father get his money back."

"Your father wouldn't risk it," Gianni says. "He's facing twenty years if the cops see him."

Emma glares at Mama Bones. "You're afraid my father will get back at you for stealing his restaurant."

"What?" Mama Bones chokes. "That horse bum old man of yours deeded me the Pardon Me against an outstanding loan two times bigger than his greasy spoon hash house is worth. You don't know nothing."

Emma lifts her chin. "I know plenty."

The redhead has another hole card to play. It's as

plain as the sneer on her face. Even Mama Bones waits for it.

"For instance," she says, "I know the Turk is planning to surround this house with a dozen men about half an hour after dawn this morning. And if they find Austin, everybody inside is going to die."

A light rain paints the sidewalk and parked cars with wet varnish, a deep coat of shine. My right hand grips my duffel bag, so I have only the left to wrap around Mama Bones' shoulders. Emma's already in the car, her Mercedes' engine running. I linger for this strangely sad goodbye.

"Thank you for saving my life," I say. "Again. And in case something happens, thank you for being a friend." I squeeze her back and kiss Mama Bones' cheek. The moisture in my eyes seems unlikely to spill, but it's there, the stuff of tears, and I wonder why I'm so despondent. Maybe it's fear. That I'd understand. I'm leaving Mama Bones, a known source of protection, for...well, Emma, a proven, completely unreliable redhead.

"You could join Vic at that very private Pennsylvania hospital," Mama Bones says. "You don't gotta go with this Emma Tierney person."

"We need to get the Turk off Luis' back," I say.

"I'm working on that."

"Yeah, but everything relates to Heriberto's murder, what I saw that night in the stables. Emma has to know something, even if she doesn't know she knows."

"Huh?"

"And maybe I can convince her to testify against Turk—like we originally planned."

"We're pretty much done talking to Turk."

I shake my head. "I have to leave, Mama Bones. I

can't get you and your nephews killed."

She squeezes my arm. "Don't use your credit cards. Watch your back."

"Goodbye, Mama Bones."

"Better watch another one of your parts, too," she says. "You know what I'm talking about, huh? In a lot of ways, you're just like Vic. Sure you don't want to spend thirty days with him in psychiatric rehabilitation?"

We stop for coffee forty minutes later and I notice Emma's right foot wiggles constantly; while she's listening, talking, even eating cheese and peanut butter-filled crackers. Our unanchored, pizza-sized table in the Garden State Parkway food court trembles like we're riding the New York subway, and I have this odd sensation I'm in a horror movie, running away from the monster.

"That night in the car, my father said he wanted to meet you," she says. "I didn't understand he was working for the Turk, that his men would kidnap you. I think you believe me or you wouldn't have come tonight, right?"

"I guess." Roll-down steel grates block every one of the Parkway rest stop's food stands. Nothing's open yet, although sounds of life emanate from a donut shop. For us and a handful of other very late travelers, it's vending machines only—coffee, candy and crackers from the breakfast robots. Wonder why this redhead likes me?

"Why did you come to Mama Bones' house to warn me? Warn us."

Emma fingers a stray lock, slips it back behind her ear. "I don't like the Turk. And I didn't want you to get killed if you were there, not after what happened at

Taki's and again in the parking lot. I felt so stupid being tricked."

"I know the feeling."

"And I wanted—maybe this sounds crazy, or stupid—but I wanted to see if you were really alive, like the Turk thought."

"You heard him say that? He knew Mama Bones was lying to him?"

"No. My father told me."

"Wait. You believed your father, even after he lied to you about wanting to meet me?"

Her blue eyes flash. "I didn't know whether to believe him or not. I said I wanted to make sure."

I lean back and sip the worst cup of coffee ever. "You're right. Maybe I'm just surprised your father's in Branchtown. You do understand he's still a fugitive, that the FBI and all kinds of law enforcement are after him?"

"What's with all the questions?"

"Lives are at stake. In particular, mine."

"My father said he's in town. I only talked to him on the phone."

Oh my. That requires further consideration. I take another sip of the world's worst java. "He came to Branchtown and didn't want to see his daughter?"

"I didn't want to see *him*."

My gaze fixes on Emma Tierney. She is not the same woman she was ten seconds ago. Her eyes hardened. Her arms wrap her own shoulders now, embracing herself.

"Are you ready to go?" she says.

Exit 63 East on the Garden State Parkway takes us toward the beach and over the Manahawkin Bay Bridge as the morning sun rises an hour later. A right turn at the next big intersection puts us on Long Beach

Boulevard. We pass a different Haven-variant village with each traffic signal. Sea Haven Crest, North Sea Haven, Sea Haven Park, Haven Beach, Sea Haven Terrace, Sea Haven Gardens and finally Sea Haven Cove, where Emma pulls her Mercedes into a gray, two-story frame house four blocks from the Atlantic Ocean. A white gravel front lawn keeps the mowers at bay, along with roped-together fake boat moorings along the sidewalk.

Inside the attached garage, Emma clicks the remote button on her car's visor for the second time. The door rattles down behind us and darkness engulfs the Mercedes' interior. Never one to miss an opportunity, I lean across the space between us, reaching for Emma's waist. The redhead meets me more than halfway, offering her face for a kiss. As our lips meet, she grips my wrist and pulls my hand to her breast. The lady is eager. My pulse jumps, and when her tongue probes between my teeth, my arousal is complete. Girl, I am so ready.

Emma's hand slides smoothly down my flank, a caress, apparently with purpose. I'm hoping she's in search of my zipper, and I wonder if the moment will fade should I suggest we move to a bedroom.

She shoves me away, hard. My shoulder bumps the passenger window.

"What's the matter?" I say.

She shakes her shoulders. Her mouth is pinched shut. "I'm sorry. I thought...thought I was ready. My doctor says...never mind."

Doctor? Oh, man, I do not want to know. But I can't help myself. "Why a doctor? What's the matter?"

She shakes me off. Is she unable to physically have intercourse? Or is she talking about a psychiatrist? Maybe she was raped, molested as a child? I remember now the newspaper hinted at something scandalous contained in Crocodile Tierney's bribery indictment. What was it?

"Let's go inside," she says.

<h1 style="text-align:center">SEVEN</h1>

As first sunlight pokes through her kitchen window next morning, Mama Bones refills Gianni's china cup with imported espresso. This handsome nephew of hers is so calm all the time, steady in the hands and eyes, the extra caffeine won't make him jumpy, even with almost no sleep. Gianni's brother Tomas, she has to be more careful. In minutes, she and her nephews could be fighting for their lives.

"How many men we have," Mama Bones says.

Gianni sits hunched over her kitchen table, his eyes glued to a black iPhone. "Four inside, four outside, four more moving around."

"Is that enough? If I don't want the Turk's men peeping around in my house, poking under the beds, we have enough guys to back me up, keep them out?"

Gianni finally glances at her, tilts his head. This way, then that way. Like he's judging a rack of Tommy Bahama shirts, which she has seen him do more than once. Half an hour one time on Lincoln Road in Miami Beach.

"If they're expecting to surprise us, yeah," Gianni says. "Turk will send two or three cars, like the Tierney woman said. Maybe ten men. But you're not thinking about refusing the search, are you? You want a gun battle outside your own home?"

"Why not?"

Gianni puts down his iPhone. He reaches for his espresso, takes a slow pull, her nephew considering his words. "Twenty-five guys throwing bullets around, one of your neighbors is going to get killed or wounded. For sure there's going to be rounds going through people's walls and windows. You agreed this wasn't the right time or place to start something serious with the Turk."

"I should let Turk send his crew tramping through my house? Peeking inside my closets and drawers, handling my dresses with their dirty hands?"

"The Turk is capo, Mama Bones. Our boss."

"This house is where my Domenic and I lived all of our marriage and raised our children. It's my home. I don't like a bunch of men coming in here and sniffing around."

"They won't find anything. Austin's gone. Turk's men will be in and out inside of thirty minutes."

"Maybe," she says. "But we've been talking and scheming about Turk for weeks, ever since he sold those children to Atlantic City. He's gotta know now I lied about them running away. That those weren't my nieces, that Smarty Pants is probably still alive. Why else is he sending men here? You know they could be coming to kill us."

"I don't think Turk's sure yet."

"It's war, Gianni."

Her nephew with the dark eyes wags his head, a curl spilling out of his hair like a young Dean Martin. "If we fight his men now it's war," Gianni says. "Better if we let them come and not find Austin. Then the Turk still won't know for sure if you're with him or against him. We'll have more time to figure the *right* time and place. Maybe we go at him this weekend, at the track."

Gianni gives her good advice. She listens to what he says. Not only are his hands and eyes steady, but her oldest nephew's head is screwed on tight, too.

"It's the safer way," she says. "But safer don't take into account the once-in-a-lifetime opportunity Turk is dumping in our lap."

"What do you mean?"

"If Turk sends ten men to search my house for Austin Carr, how many guys is he gonna have protecting him this morning?"

I almost forgot the way her body felt in my hands twenty minutes ago, but when Emma twists, stretches and squats to peer inside the beach house's white plastic kitchen cupboards minutes later, all those recent sensations return. She checks every shelf and drawer, top to bottom and front to back, spreading her thighs or shifting her hips each time. Needless to say, I can't keep my eyes off. This wild, perhaps damaged, beauty packs her fresh designer jeans like two million dollars fills out a checking account. Still, I'm glad nothing happened in her car. Emma's flat blue eyes tell me something is *definitely* off inside.

I glance away. "Did you have a nice shower?"

"Heavenly. A hundred times better than an hour of sleep." She opens and scans the near-empty freezer drawer of her refrigerator. "There is absolutely nothing in this house for you to eat—unless a frozen TV dinner sounds good."

"Ha."

"There's a deli five blocks away." She points with a finger. "Walk back the way we came in, to Bay Avenue and turn left."

I nod. "You sure your dad or someone else isn't going to drop in today? Such a beautiful beach house. It's July third and the weather's nice."

Her dark red curls flutter, shaking her head. "Nope." The beach house walls, curtains, furniture and carpet are all white. Even the kitchen knick-knacks are white porcelain, including a six-inch porpoise on the window sill. A vase with no flowers. Her red hair is virtually the only color in the room.

"My father sold this place to Aunt Barbara when he needed the money for his legal defense. She could have flipped the property for all he knows."

"What about your aunt? She must use it."

Emma shuts the freezer drawer. "Aunt Barbara hates the beach, hates the sun." Emma slips a navy blue sport coat off a kitchen chair and picks up her leather attaché case. Off to work, she warned me earlier.

"She bought this place from him to help her brother, and as an investment. I'm the one who rents the property for her, the only person in the family who's ever slept here since Aunt Barbara bought it."

"All right," I say. "I appreciate it. When are you coming back?"

"Tomorrow evening. I have a dinner meeting tonight with a client, and a busy day Thursday."

"You're in finance, too?"

"Real estate. What will you do for two days? There's a bookstore across the street from the deli. And the shore's only four blocks away. There're probably still a pair of men's swim trunks in the smaller bedroom."

"Think I'll work the phone. My lawyer needs to update me about Luis. Plus, I could actually call a few clients, sell some—"

The front door rattles. My heart crashes against my ribs.

Emma gasps and seizes my elbow as the entrance swings open.

A rifle barrel is the first object inside, then a man holding the rest of what looks like a military assault weapon. Shaved bald and thick across the chest and shoulders, he's wearing black jeans, black sneakers and a black T-shirt. My brain sees him as a deadly bug crawling toward me. My gut clenches.

The man in black shouts to someone behind him. "We have company."

I reach for Emma. The kitchen has a back door fifteen feet away. A lightly curtained window behind me. A small backyard opens onto an alley. If this Stygian soldier is going to shoot us, we need to run for our lives. But my instinct says no. This guy won't blast so powerful and loud a weapon. Not in this neighborhood. Not unless I force him.

He raises the weapon, puts a one-eyed gaze on me over the gun-sight. "Get down on the floor. Keep your hands where I can see them and away from your body."

I guide Emma from the kitchen into a more open area and onto the floor beside me. Her breathing is labored. Wheezy. Her hand trembles on my forearm. She couldn't have set this up. Odd I think that even though I have no idea what *this* is. The scene is unreal. The white walls, white curtains, white furniture and white carpet are too stark a background for the inky black gun with a foot-long ammunition clip. There should be movie cameras.

Another man comes inside, this one thinner and dressed for the beach with shorts and a white flowered camp shirt. Sandals. Could be a friendly neighbor except for the matching military-style assault rifle. I'm watching all this from a worm's perspective, the toes of my loafers on the kitchen floor, my face deep in the living room's white pile, wall-to-wall carpeting. A faint stink of ancient spoiled milk tries to add reality to this beach-house crazy, assault weapon world, but nothing could make sense after we're joined by yet another arrival, a tall and well-dressed man who closes the door behind his giant frame.

It's the Turk.

* * *

Mama Bones sits beside her double bed, her gaze on a pillow hiding the Sig Sauer. Turk's man on her balcony—the big blue son-of-a-bitch—is not looking, has his back turned. And Turk's man searching upstairs got swallowed up inside the old sewing room Gianni turned into a walk-in closet. Maybe he thinks Smarty Pants is hiding between her racks of black dresses.

Forcing herself to breathe slowly, she calculates how long it would take her to hop beside the bed, grab the fifteen-shot pistol and plug both of these mamalukes. The big gun is heavy. She needs two hands to pick it up, aim and shoot. But still she could probably get off two or three shots before either of these two turkeys fired back.

It's war now anyway. Mama Bones is pretty sure. And she's killed before. They don't call her Mama Bones for nothing. Her fingers are white against the arm of the oak chair her dead husband made long ago in his garage workshop. Took him six months to make the most painful seat in the house. Takes two cushions to use it.

She sighs. Maybe she's too upset to think clearly. Even if she did successfully shoot both of these men, what about the rest of Turk's crew downstairs? Mama Bones is angry enough to start a war, but probably not Tomas' or Gianni's men. They're not expecting a shootout now, that's for sure. Everybody knows Austin is gone.

She twists her gaze from the pillow and the temptation beneath it, instead checks Turk's man now on her bedroom balcony, the three hundred pounder wearing pale blue sweats. Matching jacket and pants. Mother Mary, even his sneakers are baby blue. He looks like a giant robin's egg.

While she watches, the big blue son-of-a-bitch reaches inside her flower pot, grabs her favorite hanging crystal pyramid, the magic one she bought at the spiritualist camp in Florida. Cassadaga.

Mama Bones pushes up from Domenic's chair and hurries outside to confront him. "Hey, get your hands off that crystal, huh? You think Austin Carr slipped away to another dimension?"

Twenty minutes later Mama Bones' ordeal is over. Turk's men are gone and most of her nephews' guys left as well. She hopes some of them are eating together right now at the Pardon Me Diner.

She sits and calls Gianni to tell him how proud he should be, how much she wanted to shoot one big guy who looked like a blue egg, but she held off. When he gets on the line, though, Gianni doesn't want to know. He don't care. He's too excited about something else.

"We followed that Lebanese fellow to Long Beach Island," Gianni says. "A private beach house. At least two men with him. Our Lebanese friend must be worried we're looking for him. It's like he's hiding."

"A private house on Long Beach Island? You're not close to Sea Haven, are you?"

"Yup. Right there. We're going to wait a few minutes, hope he comes back outside."

A cold shiver tickles the center of Mama Bones' spine. There is something very wrong. This is a feeling she got only four or five times before in her whole life. Someone is going to die—that's what happened before—and there is nothing she can do.

"I think you should call this off," Mama Bones says. "Something is wrong, I'm pretty sure."

"This fight is coming whether we like it or not,"

Gianni says. "We might as well have surprise on our side. And trust me, we've got an edge. My brother picked us up some totally shocking outfits."

Mama Bones remembers why Sea Haven rings a silver bell. "Tell me about the house in Sea Haven. This place is not a gray two-story on Iroquois?"

Gianni grunts. "You know the place?"

Oh, Mother Mary. "That house belonged to ex-mayor Croc Tierney. His sister Barbara tried to sell it to me the same time I took over the mortgage on the Pardon Me Diner. I looked at it, but the monthly nut was too big, the rental market weak."

"Maybe our friend the Lebanese bought it."

"I don't think so. You don't see an old Mercedes parked close by, do you?"

"Jesus. You mean the redhead's car? Emma's? What a long shot."

"How about the garage?" Mama Bones says. "Can you peek inside?"

"I'll call you back. There's a window. Tomas can check inside with his binoculars."

Mama Bones' heart thumps. Could Austin Carr and the Turk be hiding in the same place? One thing for sure, it wouldn't be a long shot like Gianni said.

Emma Tierney connects everybody and everything.

Two months ago, the Turk and I were toe to toe, and ever since, the gangster has been trying to shut my big mouth permanently, first with a thoroughbred filly named Zip Your Lip, most recently with Bayonne Billy Zantori and the Atlantic Ocean. The White House chef will serve poop before Turk forgets my face. So when I see my enemy Johnny the Turk Korsay walk into Emma's beach sanctuary behind two heavily armed gunmen, I stick my snoot in a sea of white rug.

Unfortunately, but not surprisingly, my simple plan doesn't work. The first guy—the man in black—takes Emma's purse and my wallet, checks our identification on the kitchen counter. "Hey, boss," he says. "This is Austin Carr."

Turk rushes to my prone body. "Big mouth?"

I did give him quite the speech the last time we saw each other. Odd, but I became nervous and overly talkative after Turk shot Luis' brother-in-law in the head.

Turk crouches over me like a wild dog. His paw rips at my shoulder, flipping me onto my back. "Your big mouth sure is quiet now."

His gaze drills me for a five count, then switches to Emma beside me on the carpet. He tugs her hair for a better look, lifting her head off the floor. My gut tightens. When Turk recognizes the redhead who dumped him for Heriberto, he releases her, letting her head snap back to the floor. She cries out.

I kick his knee. "Asshole."

Turk shouts and drops to the knee I kicked. The guy in black is on me in a flash, dropkicking my ribcage. I'm so scared and full of adrenalin, I don't feel the pain.

Emma says, "Don't hurt him, Johnny."

Turk grunts. "If it wasn't for your father, I'd kill you, too."

Turk staggers to his feet and holds out his palm toward the man dressed all in black. Turk's fingers wiggle. "Give me your gun."

Turk grabs a black semiautomatic, and Branchtown's boardwalk version of the Godfather steps directly over me, straddling my hips. A big van or truck rumbles by on the residential street outside, a grating sound that makes the skin around my eyes twitch. Why did I come back from that Mama Bones ordered vacation? I should have known she wouldn't let me leave—at least not before encountering bloody violence and death one more time. I could be lying on a sunny beach somewhere. Maracaibo is fun to pronounce. I think that's in Venezuela.

Turk aims the pistol at my nose. "You want to roll over and hide, or you want to see it coming?"

EIGHT

Bending over me, Turk polishes my forehead with his semiautomatic. My bladder shivers and threatens to empty. Clearly, I am no longer the cool cucumber I used to be when facing death. Even a few months ago I might have commented on Turk's incredibly well-made suit of clothes. Check the way those trousers fold and glide across his knees. Some fabric, too. That fancy Egyptian cotton probably. But this morning I remember the way life fled Heriberto's frightened eyes the night Turk shot him. Heriberto died staring at me, begging me to help him, and I will never be the same. My ticker's knocking so hard and fast, I could drop dead before Turk pulls the trigger.

"Tell me the truth and I'll let you live," Turk says. "Were you at Mama Bones' house last night?"

Not sure why I used to be so glib staring down gun barrels, but the old Austin Carr is dying. I'm becoming a new, less talkative man. I shouldn't say anything about Mama Bones. Not even a *no* to his question. Turk is known for reading faces, telling if someone's lying. And Turk is going to shoot me anyway. It doesn't matter whether I talk or not.

Turk points the weapon at Emma. "You want to watch her die?"

I guess my face doesn't respond the way Turk wants, so he grabs my throat and squeezes. "Tell me! Were you with Mama Bones last night or weren't you?"

Hard to answer with my vocal chords being crushed, even if I were inclined. Every square inch of me blossoms with sweat. My hands grab his arm and twist. If I knew jujitsu, judo or karate, maybe I could toss him through the back window. Alas, all I can do is breathe again, which when I think about it, is actually a pretty major accomplishment. Major but temporary. Turk breaks my grip, straightens up and tenses his finger on the trigger.

This is it, the end of Austin Carr. I hold my breath and wait.

Emphatic knocking interrupts my execution. Someone pounds with force on the beach house's solid oak front door. Whoever, they are anxious, urgent, mad or some multiple combination thereof. The walls shake. Lamps rattle.

Turk says, "Jerry, check the window. See who it is."

The guy in black remains at the kitchen counter, motionless, so I quickly deduce the guy in shorts, flowered camp shirt and sandals must be Jerry: Also, he's the one scooting toward the front picture window and the repeated loud knocking. Jerry is not as big as the Guy in Black, but he carries his assault rifle with ease and obvious experience. He crouches at the window ten feet from the entry. He uses his left forefinger to inch back the curtain.

"Two Jersey State Troopers," Jerry says. "They're holding documents."

My mouth may be failing but the luck is holding. My lips part to suck in a fresh breath of hope. The mountie-hat wearing New Jersey State Police may have saved my life. Probably trying to serve a pre-existing traffic warrant on Emma Tierney or her aunt, Barbara Ryder. Or maybe the Feds sent Jersey's two-toned blue uniformed cops to check Croc's old property, see if the indicted ex-mayor might be visiting. You know they're still looking hard for that guy. Long-outstanding Federal warrants don't buttress any reputations except Croc's.

"All right, stay cool," Turk says. "If nobody answers they'll go away."

"I don't like it," Guy in Black says. "Maybe the stockbroker told Mama Bones he was coming here."

"So she called the State Troopers? I don't think so."

More pounding on the front door, the weight of the blows jiggling the doorknob and shaking the front window blinds, altering the light filtering inside the all-white living room. Turk motions Guy in Black and his assault rifle closer to the entrance, Turk in his fancy suit pointing and showing the way like a theater usher.

"They know someone's inside," Jerry says. "Maybe I should answer—"

Explosive gunfire trashes the window beside Jerry and slams holes in the waist-high partition dividing living room from kitchen. The shots hit Jerry's torso and drive him back toward the center of the living room, one quick shot after another—like truck wheels smacking a series of speed bumps. *Bang bang bang bang.*

The series of explosions is energizing, heightening my senses, and all four walls seem to shudder when Jerry topples onto his back. His tanned feet are bare, his empty leather sandals remaining where he once stood by the window. Jerry's flowered camp shirt grows two blood-red flowers.

Turk bolts from the kitchen and runs through a corner of the living room. He disappears into the hall leading to the bedrooms with perfect timing—the moment the front door splinters and the frame bursts into pieces. The thick slab of solid oak swings loose and slams flat on its hinges against the interior wall, the white handle disappearing into the sheetrock.

Guy in Black fires his assault rifle. His bullets zip over our heads, but the spray of hot metal catches the first blue-uniformed Trooper coming fast through the broken entryway. Wounded, the Trooper jerks backward, his light-blue jacket turning purple in two or three spots. He topples against the interior wall, face first, sliding down to streak the all-white world with bright red blood.

As he crumples to the white carpet, my stomach heaves and a second Jersey State Trooper dives inside, his body no more than three feet off the carpet. His weapon fires our way. Pieces of kitchen counter fragment above Emma's head. Glass breaks behind us in the kitchen—a window or dishes, I can't tell. And I'm not sticking my head up to look.

The back kitchen door busts open behind Emma's right side and new explosions of gunfire shake my teeth. Not a rat-a-tat-tat like the movies. Each single explosion is like a bomb going off, one after another. More bullets smash the kitchen counter near Emma.

Guy in Black quits firing. His weight lands hard on the kitchen floor.

Heavy feet rush inside behind us, and the second Trooper who entered like an Olympic swimmer scrambles up into a crouch. He's not worried about bullets anymore. He levels his gun at me. From the floor, I show him my empty hands. My fingers are trembling.

A familiar voice says, "He's okay. That's Carr." I twist to see Tomas, then push myself up to face him. I think Emma and I have been rescued. I take a deep breath.

"Where's Turk?" Tomas asks.

I point to the hallway. "He ran."

Glass shatters in the back of the house. The noise is quiet compared to the gunshots that somehow linger in my ears, but Tomas, who wears Bermuda shorts and a white T-shirt, grips his pistol tighter and runs past me toward the sound. I clasp Emma's hand and lift her. Her palm is slippery wet, her eyes, foggy.

The second Trooper crouches beside the first and checks for a pulse. His shoulders visibly sag, suggesting the test results are negative. Both of these men are not real Troopers, obviously. They work for Gianni and Tomas, and by extension, Mama Bones. I'm also guessing full-boat war now exists between Turk and the Bonacellis.

Another gunshot echoes from the back of the house. Boy, do I need to get out of the Jersey bond business. The second Trooper glances at me. "Did you see anyone besides these two guys and the Turk?"

"No."

"Nobody earlier? Nobody in a car outside?"

"Nope."

Tomas jogs back into the living room from the hallway. His dark handsome face droops when he gazes at his unmoving comrade. "How's Jimmy?"

The second Trooper shakes his head. "He's gone. How about the Turk?"

"Think I winged him," Tomas says. "He ran down the alley toward Bay Ave. I'm going to chase him on foot. You and Carr get Jimmy in the van, come find me."

Tomas lopes out the kitchen door. The fake Trooper nods at me. "Come over here and grab Jimmy's feet."

Mama Bones checks her cell phone. Even in her old wooden garage with the lights out, the windows blocked, sitting in the front passenger seat of her dead husband Domenic's hot rod 1955 Chevrolet Nomad, she can read the numbers: twenty-two minutes since Gianni called to say Tomas and his men were busting inside the beach house. How much time does it take to shoot three guys, huh?

She lifts the Sig Sauer from her lap and places it beside her on the driver's seat. The thing is like holding a five-year-old: it's nice, but after a while you gotta put it down and rest. Plus, she probably isn't going to need a gun for hours. If Turk figured out right away who was behind the beach house attack, called somebody, Mama Bones would already be dodging bullets.

Probably.

She checks the cell again. Twenty-four minutes. She can't help worrying, especially about Tomas and his yogurt breakfasts. She's concerned he's not strong enough. Gianni's okay, the older nephew. He told her he's not even going inside, but staying back in the van to watch the house. As for the redhead, Mama Bones don't care one way or the next. And Austin? Smarty Pants is indestructible.

It's Tomas who could get hurt.

Twenty-six minutes.

Outside the window of Domenic's hot rod Chevy, their old disassembled and carefully wrapped dining room table leans against the garage's wood framing. Mama Bones spends Christmas with Vic and his family now, but for thirty years that rosewood dining board fed twenty to twenty-five of the combined Bonacelli and Rossi clans, including Gianni, Tomas and their sisters, their mother, Vincenza, God rest her soul, plus a dozen Bonacellis from Domenic's side. She worked for days preparing food, then cleaning pots, but Mama Bones misses those big Christmas dinners. So many of those faces are gone.

The cell phone lights up. So does her heart when she sees it's Gianni. "What happened, huh?"

"Jimmy's dead. Everybody else is okay, including that yellow Turk who ran like a mouse."

"Jimmy Jakowitz got killed?"

"Yeah."

"That's bad. At least his momma is already passed and she don't have to hear about it. So Turk took off, huh?"

"Soon as the shooting started, Carr said. Carr was inside on the floor. Tomas chased Turk into a back bedroom, fired a shot at him through the busted window, then chased him down the alley."

"Where are you?" Mama Bones says.

"We're in the van driving around, looking for Tomas."

Mama Bones bites her knuckle. "Listen, Gianni. You gotta leave that part of town. You gotta ditch that van. The neighbors probably already posted a shot of it on Facebook. Was there much shooting?"

"Plenty. People watched us leave, too. Turk's man used an AK-47 on Jimmy as he busted in the door."

Mama Bones takes a deep breath. "So how come you still in that van, huh?"

"I told you. We're looking for my brother."

"Tomas can take care of himself." Mama Bones tightens her grip on the black plastic cell. "There's a supermarket on Bay Ave—an A&P or a Shop-Rite, I can't remember—but it's about ten blocks from you. Take the van there, park behind the store. Then one at a time, you go inside, shop, fill a basket. Wait for the person I'm gonna send with new wheels to pick you up."

"Forget about it," Gianni says. "Tomas could have Turk cornered right this minute. Or Tomas could be hurt himself. I'm going to keep looking."

"No. We'll find him later, after you ditch the van."

"I've only searched one block."

"That's all you got time for, Gianni. Go to the supermarket. And don't use Bay Avenue."

"Who are you going to send? I told everybody who wasn't part of this deal to scatter. I mean everybody. We need an SUV, too, or a van."

"I could drive the Escalade down."

"No, you can't. I accidentally took the keys."

Mama Bones thinks of another possibility. "Where are the keys to Domenic's Chevy Nomad?"

"What? You haven't driven a car since Tomas and I moved in, let alone that antique, four thousand pound hot rod. There's no power steering. That big block Chevy engine Dom installed has more cubic inches than your basement."

"I can still out-drive you. Where the keys, huh?'

Waiting to find out where Gianni is taking us in the van, while I have a few minutes to think, I'm wondering if all the serious mayhem in my life is really about Mama Bones, Vic and our securities business. Showing investors how to save for the future and helping small business owners manage their employee pension programs isn't a bad way to make a living. The stock market doesn't have to be about gambling. What I'm thinking, maybe all this recent bloodshed is the result of redheads, not the Bonacellis. The last few years were one disaster after another, a body count in the dozens. And though Mama Bones or Vic always forced the violence, a redheaded woman kicked off each fiasco. Kelly Burns, the rich man's wife. Franny Chapman, the cop with a past. And Patricia Willis, the info thief who got her brother disbarred.

Perhaps a Strange and Comedic Attraction to Redheads (SCARS is a self-help group I'm thinking of starting) represents the single biggest flaw in my genetic code. Am I mentally diseased because of long recessed genes, a highly self-destructive ancestry perhaps connected to mead-swilling Vikings? It's an interesting line of thought, at least worth considering while traveling in the back of Gianni's stolen van, Emma leaning against my shoulder. To dwell on the horror and death I witnessed at Emma's beach house would be to start trembling. That Emma looks to me for strength is enough to make me stronger.

We pull into a shopping market parking lot. I heard only one side of the conversation, but enough to know Mama Bones forced Gianni and the ex-fake Jersey Trooper—Dustin, Gianni calls him—to abandon their search for Tomas. We made a beeline north and now conclude our trip by visiting a busy A&P. Further consideration of my potential genetic problems will have to wait. The van noses up against a green garbage container overflowing with cardboard boxes.

Gianni cranes his neck, stares left and right through the top of the van's windshield. "There are too many security cameras around. Suckers cover every inch of the lot. We can't get out of the car."

"Call Mama Bones," Dustin says.

Gianni shakes his head. "Maybe in a few minutes. I don't want to bother her while she's on the Parkway driving." He jams the gearshift in reverse. "We'll park someplace close."

"There's a gas station and convenience store across the street," Dustin says. "Lots of cars. And I'm out of smokes."

Gianni turns our bus around. My weight shifts against Emma. I'm in no hurry to slide away either. She snuggles even closer as we bump across the street and park behind a brown UPS truck at the back of the gas station lot. Emma's long hair tickles my neck. "Can we get something to eat?" she says. "A bag of chips or cookies?"

"Sure," I say. "Chocolate chip okay?"

She nods, completely calm. I know I'm burying the fear and the horror of what happened at that white beach house, so I'm changing my mind about Emma looking to me for strength. I'm numb from the blood and gore, weakened by an instinctive sense of loss. With Emma, it's like she had a bad day.

I look at Dustin. "What kind of cigarettes you want?"

"I'll get them."

"I'm going inside to buy Emma cookies anyway."

He fishes a ten dollar bill from a silver horseshoe clip in his front pocket. Dustin's in blue jeans now. Faded denim and a plain white T-shirt. "Marlboro reds."

I work the van's sliding door and hop onto the asphalt.

Gianni says, "I'll be pointing the other direction when you come out."

The morning sun warms my neck and arms. My leg muscles enjoy the twenty-yard stretch into the convenience store. We're only a blocks from the beach. Ocean waves break against shallow water when the noise of passing cars is interrupted.

A chilly air-conditioned breeze greets me inside the well-lighted market. The store is six aisles wide, fifty feet long, every inch packed with brightly colored products. Half a dozen other customers mill about. A vertical display of potato chips and cookie snacks beside the checkout counter draws my attention, and I snag packages of chocolate chips and pretzels.

The man behind the cash register reaches for my first item, the pretzels, and slides it over an electronic price reader. He glances over my shoulder when a refrigerator door slams, and the concerned expression on his face activates my paranoia. I reach for my wallet as an excuse to twist and look.

Headed toward us at the cash register is the Turk.

NINE

Turk stumbles toward the counter clutching two bottles of water, a roll of paper towels and black electrical tape. His cheek and chin bleed. The London-made suit jacket is torn at the shoulder, where another wound shows even more blood. His previously slicked and parted business hairdo has exploded into a stylish bird's nest. Turk's eyes widen when he sees me. His water bottles clatter to the tile floor as he reaches inside his jacket.

One good thing about my association with the Bonacelli clan, I know when an armed criminal is going for his weapon. Leaving my wallet in my back pocket and Emma's snacks on the counter, I sprint for the exit. Three strides from the glass doors, my left shoulder knocks over a display of embroidered hats, pennants and other baseball souvenirs. Philadelphia Philly mementos.

If it was Yankee stuff, I'd go back and straighten up.

The Turk's first gunshot zips past me high and to the left, eight or ten inches above my shoulder, an angry hornet on steroids. The explosion burns my ears and the bullet puts a perfect hole in the convenience store's smoky glass door.

My hands hit the door handle and frame, the latch opens and I taste fresh beach air again. My head, hips, and shoulders get halfway outside.

Turk's second shot knocks me through the open door and down onto one of those thick-woven, black rubber mats, the kind store owners wish people actually wiped their feet on. Barely breathing, so stunned am I by sound of the gunshots and pain on my left shoulder top, my mind scrambles for understanding.

Have I been shot?

Mama Bones squeezes the steering wheel with both hands—like she holds her Sig Sauer. The loud, vibrating Chevrolet station wagon is especially hard to handle at ninety miles an hour. Domenic always said the extra-stiff, hot rod suspension didn't smooth out until one-twenty.

The four-lane road clears ahead and Mama Bones chances a peek at the wallet-size rearview mirror. That's good. No more red and blue flashing cop lights behind her. Crossing the bridge onto Long Beach Island at one hundred and thirty miles an hour was risky. Barely missed a few slower cars. Plus she didn't slow enough at the intersection, nearly flipped making the turn onto Bay Avenue. But at least for a minute she's lost those two police cars.

Next block she hangs a right, then another right, slows down to a creep, not an easy thing with the big engine wanting to idle the car forward at forty miles an hour. She has to ride the brake. Domenic spent hours and whole weekends restoring the old Chevy station wagon, a Nomad they called them. He switched in a giant engine when Vittorio was in high school and had an interest in cars. But Vic—he hates being called Vittorio—Vic never touched this car or any other one after his father died.

Single-family homes line one side of the residential street, two and four-unit apartment houses the other. All the buildings sit bunched together, lined up neat like pastel colored cookies cooling on a tray. At the end of the block, by a gray two-story with more anchors in the yard than New York Harbor, Mama Bones brakes where she can barely peek around a corner at Bay Avenue—and the very same intersection she drove through one minute ago.

She didn't lose any cops. Picked up a few. Red and blue flashing lights zoom by in a fast parade down Bay Avenue. One, two, three black and white State Troopers, plus two all-white local police cars chasing her now. She bites her knuckle. How come she had to drive so fast on the Parkway, huh?

Mama Bones turns the car right again, then slides her foot off the brake. The loosey-goosey Chevy shoots forward. She needs to find a hiding place quick. An empty big garage would be nice. Someplace to get this old Chevy out of sight. What was that shop she just passed on Bay Ave?

The next street is like the first one—single-family homes lining one half, small apartment units the other. On this quiet residential avenue, Mama Bones finds a narrow alley behind the businesses fronting Bay Avenue. Pretty sure she passed a muffler shop before she made the right.

There it is. The big roll-up door is open, too. Mama Bones needs all of her arm muscles to hang the sharp left, whip directly inside the shop, narrowly missing three men in blue work overalls standing by a curbed food truck.

She keeps rolling until she's squarely parked inside a four-posted, hydraulic car lift. Checking around, Mama Bones counts two other lifts, both inside diagnostic test bays. There are a total of four workbenches, all of them with tire-changing stands, air hoses for their power tools, and wall charts with spare parts. Pretty fancy muffler shop she found.

She rolls out of the Chevy, dials Gianni while she

walks to the roll-up door and punches a red button. An electric motor whirs and the garage's steel door slides down. The men outside start talking, then hollering at her. Running even. But the door closes and she locks it. Gianni answers his phone.

"Hey," she says.

"Where are you?" Gianni says.

"Jerry's Muffler Shop in Sea Haven Cove. The cops were chasing me so I had to hide. How about you?"

Gianni takes his time answering. He makes noise, too, like he's holding back a sneeze. Laughing at her? Mamaluke.

"We're parked between two trucks in a Walmart," he says.

A bald guy in blue overalls walks up to Mama Bones. The red stitching on his chest says his name is Allan, and also that Allan is the Manager of Jerry's Muffler Shop. Mama Bones nods to Allan while she talks to Gianni. "Parked?" she asks. "You're not still in the van, are you?"

"We couldn't leave it at the supermarket," Gianni says. "The whole lot was covered with security cameras—"

"Can I help you, ma'am?" Allan says.

"—so we parked across the street at a gas station and convenience store," Gianni says. "Austin went inside. There was a holdup or something. He got shot."

"What?"

Allan says, "Excuse me, ma'am. Would you mind getting off the telephone?"

"Emma jumped out and ran to help him," Gianni says. "I couldn't stop her. She was still there nursing him when the first cops came. Dustin and I took off."

Allan says, "Ma'am? Please?"

Mama Bones holds up her finger, mouths the words

five seconds. "How bad did Austin get shot?"

"Didn't look too bad," Gianni says, "but we couldn't see much except he wasn't dead. We had to get out of there. I'm going to leave the van at Walmart and steal something new. It's what we should have done earlier instead of you driving here in that Chevy."

"Get off the phone," Allan says, "or get the hell out of my shop!"

Mama Bones keeps the phone against her ear, but steps closer to the Chevy, then reaches inside through the driver's window and grabs the Sig Sauer from her purse.

"You want us to come get you?" Gianni says.

Mama Bones points the gun at Allan. "Yeah, we might have to stay here a while."

Twelve minutes later Mama Bones lifts her knee from Allan's spine and stuffs the Sig Sauer back in her leather bag. "Try to get some rest," she says to him. "If your men are gonna take the day off, you might as well, too, huh?"

She can't understand what Allan says back. He was a good talker when she forced him to send his men home. But now the grease rag in his mouth makes his voice an angry buzz. "I promise I'm gonna send you a nice bag of cash for the lost business," she says. "Trust me."

Her cell phone rings again as she leaves, closing the door to Allan's office. The call is from Gianni. Not the one she's been waiting for.

"We're turning into the alley right now," Gianni says. "Open up."

Mama Bones shuffles to where the big red button sticks out of the wall. She pushes with the heel of her hand, a motor whirs overhead, and the big bay door rolls up into the ceiling. The sunlight pouring inside makes her squint. She sneezes as her cell phone rings again. It's Luis.

"Good timing," Mama Bones says. "Our mutual friend has been shot. If we're gonna use him like we talked about, you have to find him and rescue him, probably from a hospital somewhere near Long Beach Island. And wherever he is, the place is also crawling with cops."

"I do not understand," Luis Guerrero says. "What has happened?"

"I'm putting Gianni on to catch you up," she says. "I gotta make up Plan B and C, talk to my crew. You're still for up for Plan A?"

"I will do what I promised, of course," Luis says. "But nothing we discussed can be accomplished if Austin is severely wounded."

"Call me when you find out," she says. "I'll tell you where we are."

Hours later, Mama Bones chews a slice of brick-oven tomato pie while Gianni ushers his men into a circle near the center of the garage's grease-stained floor. Mama Bones swallows her last bite of lunch, steps into the middle of the group and spreads on the floor a map of New Jersey. She found the folded street guide in Allan's desk. "I got some 'splaining to do," she says.

Seven men push closer. They know how bad things are. Her argument with the Turk over those child sex slaves has exploded into all-out war. Men are dying, their families ruined. More deaths could be coming, too. She stares at each member of Gianni's and Tomas' crew. How much easier their lives would be if she gives Austin to the Turk and agrees to turn over those Asian girls.

"It's been thirty years since we saw fighting like this,"

Mama Bones says. "So long ago, none of you ever been in a war. That's one problem puts us on the defense. Another is that Turk has more men."

Gianni coughs. "Some of us think the problem is you, Mama Bones. You taking those girls." Gianni waves around the table. "It needs to be discussed."

Tomas nods at her.

Mama Bones shrugs. "Okay, fine. But I don't see how there's much to discuss."

"And then you hide this guy Austin Carr?" Gianni says. "Why don't you do what Turk wants? Give him the stockbroker?"

Mama Bones raises her chin. "Okay, maybe you're right. This war is my fault. But like me, how come you don't want to help little babies with no Mom or Dad, huh? What kind of man are you who doesn't want to help little girls who get kidnapped and turned into sex slaves until they die of disease? Why wouldn't you guys wanna be part of that, huh?"

To a man, gazes drop. No one will look at her now. No one except her nephew Gianni. He's their leader.

"That's not fair, or the issue," Gianni says. "There are sex slaves all over the world, not just in Jersey. You're asking us to risk our lives because of your charitable activities. That's not right. Some of us are going to die."

Mama Bones stares at her nephew. "Maybe you, Gianni. Your big mouth always gets you in trouble."

"I'm only saying what everybody here is thinking."

"Maybe nobody gets killed," she says. "My plan, we head for the fort now, stay quiet and out of trouble."

She grabs one of Allan's grease pencils, marks an X on the Jersey map. "You all know this place. How me and Gianni wired it up last winter, right? We'll stay safe there while someone I hired takes out the Turk and stops this war. Someone who came to me with a very good plan. We gonna wait for him to do his job."

Gianni frowns. "The stockbroker?"

"No," Mama Bones says. "His friend, Luis. That attorney Zimmer got him out of jail last night."

The newly remodeled emergency room at St. Thomas Medical Center resembles the set of a science fiction movie. I perch on a previously invisible gray seat that unfolds from the wall with a nurse's mere touch. The flat steel surface is no thicker than an iPhone and half the size of my butt. To be more uncomfortable, the rock-hard mini stool would have to sprout two-inch spikes.

A pea-size chunk is missing from the fleshy top of my left shoulder, and standing beside me, examining the bandage, Emma rubs my good shoulder with her hip. "If the doctor's done stitching you, shouldn't we be getting out of here?"

"Good instincts, but too late," I say. "That man and woman walking our way look like new detectives with the same old questions."

"Uh, oh," Emma says.

"What?"

"Those two work for Johnny. I've seen them at the track."

These two detectives have to be Davenport and Lindsay then, the crooked cops Mama Bones called to rescue Turk the night of Heriberto's murder. Mama Bones and Gianni told me about them at the Pardon Me, said these cops claimed to find Heriberto in a car trunk, then snatched Luis to ask him questions, possibly frame him for the murder. They said Davenport and Lindsay work for the Seaside County Prosecutor's Gambling Enterprises Unit.

The man is taller, but under six-foot. He wears his bright orange-red hair in an evenly cropped, one-inch thick mat. But it's his female partner—a sharp-faced little brunette—who holds up her gold badge, points her male partner off to stand by the back ER entrance. She wants to talk to me undisturbed.

"I'm Lieutenant Davenport with the Seaside County Prosecutor's Office," she says. "That's my partner, Lieutenant Lindsay. We need to ask you a few questions."

"Sure. But I don't think I left anything out of my earlier statement to the local police."

"Really?" She rests her hands on her hips, opening the coat of her navy blue business suit enough I can see the holstered semiautomatic pistol. Looks like a Glock. Something's wrong when small-time Jersey stockbrokers recognize a variety of deadly weapons. "I read your statement," she says. "It kind of makes sense. Kind of. But why start running because a beat-up old man is walking toward you?"

Davenport's nose seems dangerously pointed. And long, like a beak. Her penetrating dark eyes add to the hawkish appearance.

"As I mentioned earlier, the old man had a gun."

Davenport shakes her head. "No. The cashier says you bolted for the door before the old guy drew his weapon. Like you knew he was going to shoot you."

"How could I know that?"

Davenport cracks an odd smile. "Come on, Carr. Everybody knows that old man. You know the Turk when you see him, don't you?"

"Johnny Korsay? No, I've never met the man."

Sure I'm lying. I met Johnny the Turk Korsay the night Heriberto died, saw him only hours ago when he almost shot me, but I'm not ready yet to tell anybody what I've witnessed, especially these two crooked cops.

Davenport inches closer, crowding me. "You're lying, asshole."

It's hard for me to mount a good bluff upon hearing the truth about my lying. Some kind of double negative thing. But I try. I am a member of the very best class of professional liars in all of America—at least one Jersey stockbroker makes the finals every year—and so I'm working to develop a believable, plausible wad of baloney. I realize quickly that I need more time, however.

"I'm exercising my right to remain silent," I say.

"Too late for that, Tinker Bell," Davenport says. "You even signed a voluntary statement."

Yuk. Moisture sprays my cheeks. Pretty sure Lady Davenport spit on me that time. But that's nothing. Her next move, her right hand strikes like a snake, latching onto my chest, screwing my shirt onto her knuckles. Two emergency room nurses behind the central station desk glance over, then keep staring. Witnesses. I do not like being manhandled. And I don't appreciate that it's this beak-nosed Davenport character delivering my humiliation. She is a cop, however, and I must suck it up.

"I'm placing you under arrest for obstructing a police investigation," Davenport says. "Please resist so I can bust your skinny ass into pieces."

She's half a head shorter than me, and the way she's standing, I could kick her in the leg and shove her backward, tripping her easily. Basic karate takedown. But she's a woman and a cop and I wouldn't even be thinking this stuff except she's a *crooked* law officer who works for the Turk. If Davenport and her partner Lindsay get me in their car and drive away, no one will ever see me again. I know this in my gut. I see it in her eyes.

She smirks. "Where's that smart mouth of yours, Carr?"

"I've never met you before. What do you know about my smart—"

She twists my shirt tighter. "Shut up."

Agitated, Emma talks to someone at the end of the corridor. She drifted off when Lindsay and Davenport showed, but now she's speaking with a tall doctor. Wait. Is that...so out of place, but yet...Emma sees me looking, hand signals me to alert Davenport to the new man's presence.

I frown at Emma, uncertain. *You really want me to do that?*

Emma nods and repeats her signaling motions. She definitely wants me to tell the cops my friend is here. I nod okay as Davenport pulls out a set of handcuffs and motions for me to spin around.

"Are you the one who arrested Luis Guerrero?" I ask.

"That's right," she says. "He's waiting for you at county—maybe the two of you can be cellmates. The thought is so romantic."

"Are you sure Luis is still in jail?" I say. "Because that sure looks like him, standing in the hallway right there?"

TEN

Lieutenant Davenport snaps her gaze toward the wide doorway of the emergency room. Tall, dark and handsome, Luis Guerrero always snags the spotlight, but this afternoon, in a well-fitting three-piece suit, white lab coat and stethoscope, he looks like a million-dollar male model. Pivoting his head and shoulders, Luis offers Davenport, Lindsay and me a manly spectacle that includes Luis' first ever full-boat grin.

Davenport makes a loud sucking sound, jerks the handcuffs away from me and bolts toward Luis. The carrot-topped Lindsay issues a four-letter word and breaks into a run, one step behind his partner.

Luis disappears from the doorway. A rolling steel bed the size of a parade float takes his place, the patient on top of the bed covered with wires, a bag of clear liquid and a throbbing electronic box. The machine beeps ominously. The two cops are totally blocked, Davenport skidding against the patient's bed rail, handcuffs still gripped in her hand.

The cops lose more time while the patient's nurse slowly pushes the rolling bed through the ER doorway. The familiar-looking woman in a pale blue uniform really takes her time, too, milking her patient through the opening with only one hand because she's towing an empty wheelchair behind her. Davenport shouts as the bed wheel bumps the cop's bare ankle.

Lieutenants Davenport and Lindsay chase a long-gone Luis through the emergency room's parking lot exit. The nurse guides the wheelchair to my side and tells me to climb in. It's Solana, Luis' wife. I was an usher at their wedding last year.

Solana pushes me out the back exit, then leads me to a very small, very hidden parking space for surgeons: three spots, nestled tight among house-sized aluminum-colored pumps, filters and ducts. Must be heating or air-conditioning equipment. Emma and Luis are waiting in a sloped-back silver Mercedes with M.D. plates, the car snuggled against a particular noisy air grate. Luis is driving.

Solana leans inside the Mercedes to kiss her husband. I watch long enough to see their lips press together, then hop in the back. My gunshot wound is small, less than a square inch of missing skin and muscle, the doc said, but I wouldn't feel much if I'd lost my arm. I am flying high from escaping certain death. Those two cops Davenport and Lindsay had murder on their mind.

A new collared dress shirt rests beside me on the Mercedes' tan leather seat. The white cotton material is still wrapped in the manufacturer's plastic.

I untie my green patient's robe.

Thirty minutes later we're pulling inside Jerry's Muffler Shop in Sea Haven Cove. In automobile garages and muffler shops, I expect cars, electronic diagnostic equipment, those big red tool chests and oily rags. Not behind Jerry's wall-sized door that rolls up into the ceiling. Instead, Gianni, Tomas, Dustin and six other men are cleaning shotguns, rifles and pistols.

Packages of ammunition are stacked on benches. A few Jersey State Trooper uniforms, one of them bloody, are piled on the floor, and armored vests are stacked inside a wooden crate. Could Mama Bones be planning armed combat?

I can only guess my role. Maybe she wants me to sell war bonds.

Three of us shinny out of the silver Mercedes, Gianni waiting by my door in a black and gray Tommy Bahama camp shirt that makes him look especially thick in the chest. He directs me by tilting his head, a chunky strand of black hair falling across his forehead. He says, "Mama Bones wants to see you."

My gaze follows his lead to a steel-framed cubicle on the south wall of the gym-size garage. I start walking. Glare from the overhead lights makes it difficult to see through the office's rectangular window, and Mama Bones' outline takes shape slowly. She's perched at a messy desk, her back to the window, the office door closed. I knock.

"Come on in, Smarty Pants."

The tiny room smells of engine oil and stale coffee. I'm guessing the middle-aged man on the couch owns the muffler shop. Poor bastard. He wears duct tape on his wrists and ankles, a name tag that says *Allan*. There's no gag. He can speak if he wants, but the expression on his face says he's pretty much had enough of everything.

Mama Bones says, "Bet you peed your pants when you saw Luis in the hospital, huh?"

"Almost," I say. "Is he cleared of the murder charges? I forgot to ask him on the way over."

"No physical evidence, the lawyer Zimmer said. They couldn't hold him anymore." Mama Bones reaches inside her black purse, a carryall dwarfing many suitcases, and renown throughout Branchtown for its exotic contents. Personally, I've seen her produce from the bag an oversize Sig Sauer semiautomatic, a Bill Clinton-engraved, gold-plated corkscrew and a perfume bottle filled with magic love potion. I sigh with relief when the pint bottle in her hand carries a familiar blue and white label.

"You wanna a sambuca?" she says.

"Why not."

Mama Bones turns to her captive on the sofa. "You want one?"

He shakes his head.

Mama Bones waves a hand at me. "Get a couple of those paper coffee cups behind you."

On a square folding card table with a twelve-cup coffee maker, napkins and a basket of sweeteners and artificial creamers, two stacks of plastic-coated paper cups zigzag toward the ceiling.

"How's your gunshot wound?" Mama Bones asks.

"I'm woozy from the medication," I say. "But I was lucky."

"You don't look so good."

"I don't feel so good. That Lieutenant Davenport scared the crap out of me."

Mama Bones pours three sambucas. She picks one up, says to Allan, "If I cut you loose—your feet and hands—you gonna run and make me shoot you in the back?"

Allan shakes his head, and I can't help but feel sorry for the guy. Since this whole day has been one gigantic disaster in reaction to the Turk's sudden and surprising aggression—as foretold by Emma—I can't imagine we all ended up at Allan's muffler shop for any other reason than his bad luck.

Mama Bones finds a pair of scissors on the desk and cuts Allan loose. "So how much I gotta pay to make up for shutting you down today?" she asks. "Five thousand cover it?" She helps a wobbly Allan to a chair by the coffee table. "Plus my Chevy wagon needs painting—the '55 Nomad I drove in. You do paint jobs?"

He nods. "Sure, but that's a classic car. You need a

fancy paint job to get maximum value."

"Oh, you like it, huh? Maybe you'd like to buy it?"

"If you're serious about reimbursing me, maybe we can work something out. What's under the hood?"

Mama Bones puts her gaze on me. "Let's talk later."

"Great," he says. "I figured you were going to kill me."

She hands him a paper cup of sambuca. "Make yourself some coffee if you want, Allan, but I think the sambuca will do you more good."

She pushes me toward the sofa. "You lie down a few minutes, Smarty Pants. You look like a corpse."

I do what I'm told, and my body discovers I am happy to oblige. "What's with all the artillery?" I say.

"It's war with you-know-who, what do you think, huh?"

"Tonight?"

"No, but we gotta move, be ready," she says. "We leave pretty soon."

"Can I ask you something?" I say.

"Sure."

"This war is about me, isn't it? You stopped the guy whose name you don't want to mention, kept his man from killing me on the boat that night. But he found out you lied to him and now it's war, right?"

Mama Bones waves off the idea. "You got some ego, Smarty Pants. Maybe you brought it on quicker, but that man and I are trouble for fifty years. This spring he heard I don't like his girl-selling business, that behind his back I'm trying to help them, especially the ones with babies. You know Luis and I have been doing that for years. Helping Mexican children with no parents?"

"No, I didn't know that."

"I figured maybe Luis told you something. Me, Luis and Solana help out in an underground group that brings sick kids to America. I'll tell you later. What's important, this war isn't about you. It's between me and the big man—a war that's gonna get bloody, unless Luis' plan works."

"What plan?"

"I'll tell you later."

That evening I realize I've been down this road before. Deep inside south Jersey's Pinelands National Reserve, a twisted forest of scrawny yellowed conifers, a now-dead local crime boss named Bluefish built himself a hotel-sized vacation lodge. A Taj Mahal of log cabins. I spent a night there two years ago, running and hiding from a highly unpleasant man I called the Creeper, and the Pine Barrens and Bluefish's lodge often haunt my dreams.

Mama Bones and Luis share the middle—a second row of bucket seats inside Gianni's black Escalade. Gianni drives, Tomas beside him; Emma and I sit on the rear bench. The six of us are, and have been, driving in total silence. The wheel-hum of the Parkway and then this two-lane county highway kept everyone quiet. Now that I'm sure where we're going, however, I've had enough of that. I touch Mama Bones' shoulder. "We hiding at Bluefish's?" I ask. "The Turk *has* to know about this place."

"Sure he does," she says. "I made him help pay for some improvements."

"You're kidding."

"Heck, no. I told him he had to if he wants to keep having Easter picnics here. You should *see* the crowd of Korsays that show up."

"All due respect, Mama Bones, Bluefish's hunting lodge doesn't seem like a great hideout if the Turk uses it regularly. Why wouldn't he just send an army to overwhelm us? We're in the middle of nowhere."

"He might, but I don't think so. He heard about all the new security I put in after Bluefish died and how much money got spent. But he doesn't know half of what Gianni and Tomas installed, how the stuff works. Plus, what makes us safe, the Turk *knows* he don't know. He could lose a lot of men."

"Does he care?"

"Sure, he cares," Mama Bones says. "He's not the President, sending out a team of Navy SEALS, guys lining up to die for their country. Turk's got a son, nephews in his crew, like me."

"Here we are," Gianni says.

Bluefish's lodge appears as I remember: a log cabin for vacationing millionaires. On a stone foundation, fifty-foot lengths of redwood planking form three separate, two-story structures—a rectangular center building, with a main entrance, then two identical square wings, one on each side. White-painted dormers and trim; cream-colored awnings on all two dozen windows.

Laid tip to tip, tar-soaked telephone poles outline the perimeter of a gravel parking lot the size of an urban gas station. The Escalade's tires squish to a stop. It's thirty yards to the front porch steps. Crows squawk in a nearby tree.

Mama Bones grabs my elbow when we scramble out of the SUV. She tugs me into the middle of the lot, away from the rest. A breeze stirs, bringing the smell of dry pine needles. It's almost dark now, the day departing; nothing left but a thick strip of pale blue on the northwestern horizon.

"When this is over, whatever happens," she says, "you and I will sit down and talk numbers. Vic and I gonna buy you out."

"You talked this over with Mr. Vic?"

"Sure. The sanitarium has a nice coffee shop."

"It's good you can joke about it."

"What else am I gonna do, huh?" Mama Bones heads toward Gianni. "Vic will be fine."

I check my surroundings and notice a new addition—a ten or twelve-foot high chain link fence topped with barbed wire. It's green and camouflaged, placed inside the tree line more than fifty yards from the house. But it's too solid a structure to miss if you're looking closely.

ELEVEN

Mama Bones sips her espresso. Stars shine in the sky like pearl buttons, but the view from the lodge's second-floor balcony is mainly pointy tree tops, shadows against the forest night. At least the air is fresh and cooler than inside. The wicker furniture reminds her of home, too.

Gianni coughs beside her.

"What?" she says. "You still want to attack?"

"I think we're making a mistake, yes. The Turk's weak. He's been shot and he's lost men. New York isn't going to support him. We should go after him, not hide."

Mama Bones lets go of her espresso, the glass cup shattering near her nephew's feet, spilling liquid on his black work shoes. Thirty years ago, when her husband Domenic ran this family, not even his best captain would say something like that. Tell Domenic he was *hiding?*

"Maybe you're hiding," Mama Bones says. "I'm going after him. Luis is leaving in fifteen minutes."

"Luis is only one man, and we have tougher."

"Luis would kick your ass in a minute."

"Maybe," Gianni's says. "Maybe not. But Turk's not going to let any outsider get close. How is Luis even going to find the Turk?"

Mama Bones stares at her nephew. It's his job to push her, make her think of other ways and see new problems, but sometimes he doesn't sound respectful. More because she's a woman than anything else, probably.

"Luis has a plan," she says. "And if Luis doesn't get Turk quick, then we do things your way. Both barrels. I don't see what's your problem letting Luis try. He has a pretty good idea."

"I don't know. Forget it." Gianni stretches his arms high above his head.

"You going to bed?" Mama Bones says.

"I guess. I've got an early watch."

"Send Austin up, okay?"

Gianni leaves her alone on the balcony. Mama Bones unconsciously reaches for her espresso. Ha. She's so tired tonight, she could probably brew herself another pot, drink the whole thing. But no use chancing it. She needs rest, has a hard time sleeping with Vic in the rehab hospital, this war with Turk, and so many unwanted girls with babies.

Austin creeps in her bedroom like a cat. Careful, nervous, checking everything before each new advance. He takes fifteen seconds to find her on the balcony. As usual, Smarty Pants is wearing his big grin.

"Hi, Mama Bones. Gianni said you wanted to see me."

She stares until he quiets down and focuses. Then she points at a wicker cabinet with a lamp on it. "Open that little door there, get out the bottle and two glasses. Let's have a sambuca, huh?"

Austin does as he's told, comes back with everything, pours the licorice-flavored syrup into crystal glasses.

She holds up her glass. "To another day above the ground." She touches her rim to his, lets the sambuca burn her throat. But the sweetness is good, the licorice flavor even better. "So you sure you wanna split up Bonacelli Investment Corp?"

"One hundred percent. Heriberto was the last straw."

"Well, it's a good thing 'cause New York says you gotta go anyway."

"Me? Personally?"

"Yeah. I would have told you before, if I'd known you were ready to sell. I was afraid you would think me and Vic were forcing you out."

"Why does New York want me gone?"

"Same reason Bluefish tried to take over two years ago. So they can launder money."

"How, exactly? Financial scrutiny gets tougher every year."

"A hundred ways, some even Smarty Pants don't know."

"You think?"

Mama Bones grins. "At least one or two."

"Are you going to buy me out at a fair price?" Austin asks.

"Let's have another sambuca, huh?"

"Sure," Austin says. "I wouldn't pass up a drink with my favorite girl."

Mama Bones laughs. "We start talking money, negotiating a price, I pour the booze...Smarty Pants pours on the charm."

Mama Bones and I agree on a general number and an independent audit to arrive at the final price. We shake and I head downstairs where Emma and Luis both want to speak with me. I don't feel like talking, so I wave them off, pretend I need to use to the restroom. I slide through a noisy, great-smelling kitchen with Gianni, Tomas and a handful of other guys eating pizza, then outside the back kitchen door to a balcony that runs completely around the lodge's ground level.

Bright roof lights illuminate a green weedy lawn that needs cutting. A warm wind rustles the pine trees on the far side of the clearing, then arrives on the porch and clings to my skin like peach syrup. A gob of self-pity chokes me. How in the hell did I get myself into this mess—dead-ass center of a war between two crime families? I try to spit, but my mouth's as dry as burlap. I haven't smoked in seven years, but a cigarette sounds delicious.

I think of a better self-soother, use my cellphone to call my daughter Elizabeth's number in Miami Beach. My ex-wife finally married the dentist she's been dating, and the whole family is on a two-week honeymoon in Florida. Elizabeth's in a happy mood when she answers, my teenage daughter having spent a wonderful night carousing with other teenagers on Lincoln Avenue. We chat a few minutes, she puts her brother Ryan on, and he gets me laughing right away. Seems my ex-wife and the dentist had a bit of a screaming match inside one of Miami Beach's fanciest restaurants.

Ten minutes later I walk back inside Bluefish's lodge feeling a whole lot better. Always the gentleman, Luis hangs back when I find him and Emma still waiting for me. Luis' manners demand he let the woman speak first.

Emma leads me into a child's empty bedroom under the stairs, her hand clammy, her eyes avoiding mine. Red and blue cartoon characters adorn the upholstered headboard and matching bedcover, but that doesn't stop Emma from wrapping her arms around me. She presses her mouth into my neck. "I want to make love," she whispers.

Her body heat works through my new cotton shirt, but an icy shower splashes on my back. "Then why are you crying?" I ask. "People should be happy when they make love."

I untangle myself and gently push her away. Her eyes overflow with tears. Her lips tremble.

A fist knocks on the bedroom door. "Our time is now," Luis says. "We must go."

"Go where? What are you talking about?"

My thoughts are on Emma's tears. What the hell did someone do to her? Was it her rat bastard father, the ex-mayor?

Luis pushes into the bedroom. "I will explain as we travel," he says. "Come. The time is now."

On a Honda motorcycle, two of us hurtling north on the Garden State Parkway, me clinging to Luis like a cashmere sweater, the wind spreads my glum expression into a full-boat grin. Though I left behind a troubled woman and a lot of friendly guns, getting out of Bluefish's creepy hunting lodge feels right. Something about the wind in my face only hours before Independence Day.

Soon, however, I realize a startling truth: this deafening combination of motorcycle engine, crashing wind and casino bus traffic make Luis a liar. There's no way he can *talk* to me, let alone explain where we're going, or what we're going to do when we get there. All I pulled from him as we mounted the bike was our goal. We're going after the Turk.

Okay, but why do we need a motorcycle?

To put things mildly, Luis' behavior causes me concern. Calling him a liar isn't much of an exaggeration. But any kind of misstatement is not like my favorite bartender. "I will explain as we travel" is exactly what he said. But there's no way he could live up to that promise, and he knew it when he spoke. That scares me. Are we headed where I wouldn't have agreed to go? On a mission I wouldn't have chosen to undertake? Maybe I jumped from a snake pit into a bear cage.

Wind catches the sleeves of my jacket, puffing up the material around my arms and shoulders like a parachute. No wonder those biker gangs look so buffed and tough. It's the air-enhanced muscles. My bones prickle from the engine's vibration, a jackhammer from foot to skull. Burnt oil and exploded gasoline push petro-stink up my nose as we fly north up the Parkway.

Luis' chest and rib muscles harden in a single contraction. He was tense before, my arms tight around him like breath-measurement apparatus, but now his flesh—his whole being—resists my grip like the hood of a car. Cold steel.

Something's wrong.

Luis brakes the motorcycle hard, throwing my weight against him, pressing air from my lungs. The bike seat lifts beneath us, tilting me forward, pressing my two hundred pounds even harder onto Luis' back. I struggle to breathe as we skid and twist sideways in an uncontrolled slide, a steel sled burning rubber underneath. The blue smelly smoke surrounds us.

The bike's rear tire catches traction and we slow at a faster rate, pitching me off balance and pushing my weight sideways. My grip slides on Luis' leather jacket. Hornets zip past my head and shoulders, and by the third one I realize they're bullets—gunshots popping like distant cherry bombs above the steady hum of Parkway traffic. Luis saw the shooters coming and saved our asses by throwing the bike into this slide. Looks like Bluefish's scary old hunting lodge was the safer place.

A dark Lincoln squeals slowly by in the lane on our left. His tires are smoking, too, but the big four-door weighs too much and can't cut speed as quickly as our motorcycle. Blue smoke fogs the space between our vehicles. One man shoots at us through the Lincoln's backseat window. A second gunman—Kalinski—fires from the front passenger seat.

My grip finds new strength on Luis' jacket.

The cloud of burnt rubber envelopes us as we stop in a sideways position, a halted target on the Parkway. Before I check to see what's coming, or have time to worry about it, Luis gooses the accelerator and we dart across two lanes of northbound traffic at a right angle. I feel like a squirrel, breaking for the trees. The momentum and the wind yank at my right arm, throwing my hand out behind me like a tiny pink flag.

More gunshots. No hornets this time, but zooming past me like a jet, doing eighty in the fast lane, a blonde on the telephone in a white Audi misses our motorcycle and my flailing hand by six inches.

Probably a good thing she never saw us.

On the Parkway's grass median, Luis brakes hard, twisting us sideways to the motorcycle's momentum and using the rear wheel to cut into the landscape like a dragging anchor. Jersey's Garden State Parkway sports a well-kept center lawn—a buffer that expands to twenty yards at this spot in the highway. Luis chews up eighteen of them before we reach a complete stop.

Twenty minutes later, when Luis flips off the motorcycle's engine one block from the ocean, my blood still pumps with adrenaline. Before the bullets started flying, I worried about Luis keeping secrets, and nothing's changed. In fact, the unknowns are growing by the minute. We needed his motorcycle to reach the sand, drive along the beach a hundred yards, then climb a narrow walkway alongside the Pink Osprey Hotel, Branchtown's notorious beachside spa. Notorious because Bluefish's predecessor and two other men were murdered in the lobby twenty years ago. I can't imagine why Luis brings us here, let alone why he needs to hide our approach.

He kickstands the motorcycle in a six-car parking lot behind what looks like the hotel's kitchen. We're closed in on three sides, and there are as many green trash bins as there are vehicles: I count five of each. Steam puffs steadily from a vent above the stained and battered kitchen door.

Luis dismounts. "I must do something tonight that causes me torment...*un dolor en el corazon.*"

His words kick up my already drumming heart. I've heard that Spanish phrase before. It means "a pain in my heart."

"But all is at stake, my friend," Luis says. "My business, my wife, the child to be borne to us this winter."

"Solana's pregnant? That's great news, Luis. Wonderful. Congratulations."

Before the words finish exiting my lips, I get a sketchy feeling about Luis' speech. Sounds like he's saying, whatever he's planning will hurt him more than it hurts me, Austin Carr. Worrisome sentiments for Luis to have. In my gut, I can't believe Luis would ever do me harm. He's saved my life so many times, it would take me five or ten minutes to make a list. Still, it might be time to remind him of our close personal relationship.

"I'd love to be the baby's godfather, Luis...I mean, if you'd like me to. You know I really enjoyed being in your wedding."

Luis waits patiently while I roll off the bike. I try a cool dismount to match his, but I'm nervous and my leg flails awkwardly. While I'm off balance, staggering on one foot, Luis kicks my weight-bearing leg, knocking me to the ground.

When I try to stand up, he punches me hard on the jaw.

TWELVE

Mama Bones flips her pillow but the new side is no cooler than the old one. She sighs. When is she going to learn to stop drinking too much espresso after dinner, huh? The sambuca is bad enough, biting holes in her stomach, like those Amazon jungle fish she saw on television. But she always adds to her—

Outside, a funny thumping sound gets loud. Moving closer. It's a strange noise, reminds her of that old Vietnam movie with Bobby De Niro and Chris Walken. Chop chop chop chop. That helicopter war movie.

Oh, Mother Mary. A chilly finger pokes Mama Bones' gut. The digit is boney and sharp, like a dead hand reaching out from the grave. Helicopters could fly over every warning and defensive system she and Gianni ever thought of.

Mama Bones sits up in bed. "Gianni! Wake up, Gianni!"

In her window, lightning streaks through the blackness like a ball of fire from a Roman candle. Then the night outside explodes in a ball of flames. Glass breaks. Wood shatters. The queen size bed she lies on lifts from the floor. A thundering roar and rushing air push Mama Bones up up up...toward dizzy blackness.

Fat Johnny, you bastard!

Pain zaps me like a blue-flash electric shock, like I plugged a frayed cord into a loose wall socket with wet hands and feet. I'm flat on my back again. And stunned. Stupefied. I can't understand. My sense of right and wrong has vanished. Luis kicked me and then hit me in the face? No way.

"Get up," Luis says.

My mouth falls open. I can't get enough air. Oxygen barely exists in this new world—gone with all reason. The salty taste of blood sours my taste buds with bitterness. That was some punch. A voice in the back of my brain says this cannot be happening, but if Luis didn't slug me, why am I bleeding?

Luis clasps my shirt and yanks me off the ground. I can't be an easy package to handle. I'm almost dead weight. On my way up, getting a view around Luis' hip, some kind of cowboy businessman exits the kitchen doorway. I assume it's a kitchen because of the steam coming out a vent above the door.

Luis shakes my shoulders, his fingers digging like claws. "Stand up."

Geez, I thought I was. Standing, I mean. But maybe my knees are buckling. I might be in shock, or confused by the cowboy heading our way. He wears a western blue suit, a western-cut white shirt and a black string tie notched around his neck with a chunk of turquoise.

Luis smacks my cheek, then tugs again on my armpits. The slap helps me focus on doing what he wants—stand on my feet.

"This is him?" Cowboy says. "Mr. Big Mouth?"

In Jersey everyone has a nickname.

Luis grunts, then wrenches my shoulders so I face the alley door. He takes most of my weight. Luis punched me harder than Kalinski. I'm still not making sense of anything. Luis and I are pals.

Unless...

"Seems like a waste of time taking this asshole inside," Cowboy says.

Luis ignores him and walks me toward that kitchen

door with a steam vent over it. By carry, I mean half dragging me, half being my crutch. Whatever he calls it, Luis supports my stumble-shuffle as we cross the asphalt. I hear Atlantic Ocean waves break against the hotel's rock barrier.

"There's nobody around," Cowboy says. "Let's do him here, stick him in my trunk." He points to a black Lincoln Town Car, one of the five in the back alley lot.

Nothing makes sense here unless Luis and Mama Bones sold me out to make peace with the Turk. My body wants to collapse from the thought. I'm tired, sore and emotionally distraught. Not to mention scared. All the other stuff that happened to me this week? It's chocolate candy compared to having Luis turn on me.

A roly-poly guy in a white apron, a white T-shirt and a white bandana around his head—looks like a cook—squeezes outside through the kitchen door. He stands in the opening, blocking our path. Live music starts with a drum roll high above us from The Pink Osprey's fifth-floor sky room.

The cook reaches inside his jumbo apron pocket. Luis's neck and shoulder muscles tighten. But the guy pulls out a box of Marlboros and a plastic lighter. He shows the red and white pack of cigarettes to us like it's a badge. "Want one?"

Luis lurches forward, forcing the cook aside and hauling me through the doorway. I expect ovens and burners—a kitchen—but the big room off the alley contains vehicles: two new, four-door Mercedes, both black, a red Ferrari sports model and a black Ford 350 pickup. All of them face a fifty-foot steel workbench against the wall. Luis' hand darts for something at our end of the workbench. A shiny tool.

"I told you we should do this jerk in the alley," Cowboy says.

He might be talking to Luis, but I'm still wondering when the roly-poly cook steps inside the room behind him. The two of them block the doorway, our only detectable exit. Each of them holds a semiautomatic pistol.

"Now I gotta do you, too," Cowboy says.

Luis eases away from me. "Senor Korsay was to meet me personally."

Is Luis telling the truth? That explains things.

"The Turk had to run," Cowboy says. "Something about an assault on a hunting lodge."

Surprise runs through Luis like an explosive charge. I feel his skin humming. "This attack you speak of must come without your *patron's* knowledge. He gave me his word."

"Oh yeah, it's with his knowledge, Senor Guerrero. His orders, in fact," Cowboy says. He switches his aim. Now I'm the guy with the gun pointed at his heart. "You first Mr. Big Mouth. Get down on your knees."

I wilt to the cement floor and wait for death like evening waits for total darkness. Dignified resignation. It's been a decent life, my two kids, Beth and Ryan, easily the best part. I'm philosophical because I'm so tired and battered, I can't even consider fighting back. I think it's because of Luis. My favorite bartender turned on me. He's willing to hand me over to the Turk so he can smooth out his own life, protect his unborn child and help Mama Bones settle with her capo.

Oh, hell. Where is that bullet?

My eyes are closed when something bigger than a bullet slashes the air. Sounds like a helicopter. My eye blink open. Cowboy's gun falls to the floor. His hands clutch his throat, fingers failing to hold back a pulsing stream of blood. The cause of his wound is a stainless-steel chisel, no doubt the tool Luis snagged from the workbench. It glistens now between Cowboy's bloody fingers, imbedded in his neck.

As Cowboy topples, the roly-poly cook runs out the doorway. His feet skip the steps and land side by side, a heavy fat slap on the pavement. Luis hurries to the doorway behind him, aims Cowboy's weapon, but doesn't fire. He lowers the weapon, checks left and right, then waves me to follow him. The change in Luis drains tension from my body.

When we climb back on the motorcycle, Luis hands me Cowboy's semiautomatic, says, "There will be shooting on the way out."

He calls Mama Bones. While he's waiting for an answer, I stare at the weapon in my hand. Guns frighten and intrigue me at the same time. They are terrible tools, of course. But if he handed me the weapon, Luis and I are back on the same side. Right?

"There is no answer," Luis says. "I left a message. Remove your belt, *por favor*."

I touch Emma's number on my cell. To Luis, nonchalant, I say, "I thought you were turning me over to the Turk."

"We will talk later," he says. "Now do as I say, quickly. Your belt, please."

There's no answer from Emma either. I leave a voice message for her to get the hell out of that lodge, and why, then slip my fake alligator belt through the loops of my trousers. Luis weaves my belt through his own once, in the back, and my belt now hangs off him like a short rope.

"Climb on the motorcycle with your back to my back," he says, "then place your belt around your waist again, tying yourself to me."

The picture appears in my head and I mount his motorcycle the way Luis wants. It's not easy: a lot of twisting, and my limbs feel like soup, but finally I'm buckled to my favorite bartender. The heels of my shoes find an edgy grip, and when I'm as balanced as possible, I grip the semiautomatic with both hands. For the next leg of our journey, call me Mr. Rear Gunner.

Luis revs the Honda once, then burns rubber busting us out of the back parking lot. We zip through the narrow alley doing forty miles an hour and exit onto a side street at right angle to the traffic on Ocean Avenue. The Pink Osprey's lobby glistens with thousands of pea-size white lights.

Movement. The back of a bakery truck swings open. Luis can't see the men inside, one crouched, the other on his belly, but I'm already lining my gun on them. Both aim extra-long, noise-suppressed pistols at us.

I carefully site the semiautomatic Luis gave me, aiming between the two baseball caps and squeeze off two shots. A shower of sparks flies from the truck's bumper. One man ducks. The guy stretched on his belly fires. I see two, then three flashes, but it's no sweat. Just more hornets. I fire once again before Luis whisks us out of range.

Mama Bones dreams about the shore, the boardwalk and old Asbury Park, the beach town she knew as a little girl, summer fun on the umbrella-covered beach. So hot in July the sand could burn your feet. She dreams of chasing her sister Vincenza inside the round green building with wooden horses and elephants, the copper dome with a carousel inside.

"You okay?" someone asks.

The Turk? Sure, Johnny Korsay rode the carousel with them sometimes. Mama Bones remembers Johnny back then. Big. Even at ten years old Johnny was too fat to scramble onto most of the wooden animals. What was that one creature low enough for Johnny Korsay?

"Wake up," the voice like Gianni's says. "It's me. The Turk hit us with freaking rockets."

Mama Bones opens her eyes. It's so dark. "Gianni?"

"Yeah, it's me. Are you all right?"

Mama Bones pushes up on her elbows. Her body is sore and tender. Scratches cover her right arm. Her aching back feels like she single-handedly unloaded a truck full of fifty-pound cement sacks. She remembers one more thing about the carousel—Fat Johnny the Turk could only ride on the alligator.

"Where are we?" she says.

"The safe room me and Tomas built. It's kind of the basement kitchen you wanted, underground, remember? But we dug a tunnel seventy-five feet from the lodge for security. I showed you the plans last year."

"Some second kitchen," she says. "That's a long walk with a twenty-six pound turkey."

Gianni shrugs. "Tell me about it. I dragged you out here. But the place has already come in handy as a safe room, you have to admit."

Mama Bones squints. She can see the room they occupy, but not too much. Steel shelves of water bottles and canned soup. The chemical toilet. Smells like her neighbor's compost heap. A dirty dungeon is what this place is, not a kitchen.

Gianni grabs her hand, wants to pull her onto her feet. "We can't stay," he says. "I thought the lodge was going to burn down, but the fire's out. Turk's men will find the tunnel soon. We don't have much time."

"How can you see if the lodge is burning or not, huh?"

Gianni points to a monitor Mama Bones didn't notice before. The screen shows three square pictures and one black box: images of Turk's men searching the rubble, the entrance to the lodge and a shot of the parking lot; and one broken camera.

"These are live pictures," Gianni says. "They're already looking for us."

Mama Bones sighs. Things are not working out so good. "I should have listened when you said the lodge wasn't safe. I didn't think about helicopters."

Gianni shrugs. "Nobody thought of missile-armed helicopters. That's James Bond crap. But it doesn't matter now. We have to get out of here."

Mama Bones lets go of her nephew's hand. She rolls onto her side, then all the way over onto her hands and knees, doggie style. Slowly, one hand on her aching hip, she leans back. Sharp pains stick her between the ribs. She hopes she didn't break anything.

"Where's Tomas?" she says.

"I don't know," Gianni says. "I thought I saw him on the monitor once after the two explosions, but—"

"There were two missiles?"

"At least. But I can't be sure it was Tomas I saw. It could have been one of Turk's men. That was ten minutes ago."

Mama Bones tries to stand, but her legs are cement. She glances up at her nephew and this time she takes his hand. The cracks and pops her bones make on the way to standing sound like milk being poured on a bowl of rice cereal.

"You okay?" Gianni says.

"No, I'm not okay. I'm pissed."

Gianni nods. "We got our ass kicked. We have to regroup."

"I'm not leaving without Tomas." Mama Bones shuts her swollen eyes. Nothing left but prayer. Except for Gianni, her most trusted men are wounded, captured or scattered. Luis and Smarty Pants are probably dead, seeing as how Turk attacked instead of going for Luis' bait. What she needs is more men. More men with bigger guns.

"Please," Gianni says. "We need to go."

"Give me your cell phone," she says. "Mine's lost."

He hands her his BlackBerry, says, "I already tried calling Tomas. There's no answer. I did get Tommy Tunes back home, though. He's coming to pick us up down by the highway. But...hey, Mama Bones, the battery's almost dead. I was saving—"

She punches three numbers.

"What's your name and what's your emergency?" the nine-one-one operator asks.

"Help," Mama Bones says. "We got shot by a helicopter."

THIRTEEN

Jersey hosts a double sunrise this Independence Day morning. There's the regular dawn, a reddish orange fingertip burning underneath the northeast sky. And then there's a Fourth of July special, the red glow over our destination in the Pinelands, Bluefish's lodge. Emma, Mama Bones and her crew must already have been attacked when we called. My concern about them all manifests itself as a throbbing pain where Turk shot me.

But I'm also worried about Luis. For only the second time since I've known him, his motives are not one hundred percent clear to me. Yes, he agreed to stop our motorcycle ride on Highway 497 so I could urinate, and yes, he's letting me carry the semiautomatic. But he punched in the face not more than an hour and a half ago. Brown pine needles crackle under my shoes as I walk back to Luis and the motorcycle.

"Thanks for pulling over," I say. "Ready to get back on the road?"

"I believe we need to talk, do we not?"

I nod. "I'd like to hear you say turning me over to the Turk was a trick, not a plan that didn't work."

Luis' eyes are black holes, absorbing everything, reflecting nothing. "If it was only a trick, why did I not warn you? Why did I strike you in the face?"

That's not what I expected him to say. Moisture forms in the palms of my hands. "I figure you needed me to *be* scared, not *act* scared. The Turk would want to see me sweating."

"But why did I speak of a pain in my heart?"

"For the same reason. To make me think it was true."

My favorite bartender smiles. He extends his right hand toward me. "Give me the gun, *por favor.*"

Mama Bones sneers at the black mesh grate and the smooth rear door panel where a four-door's latch and window crank should be. The back seat of this cop car looks, feels and smells like a jail. A scary thing for women. Even scarier since these two cops belong to the Turk. Makes her want to puke. Gianni was right when he said she made a big mistake telling the nine-one-one lady their location.

"All the cash I send your way Christmas, you think you could get this pile of junk washed," Mama Bones says. "Smells like urine and throw-up back here."

"Shut up, you shriveled old bitch," Davenport says.

The man Lindsay is driving. He says, "Don't exaggerate, partner. She's not that old."

Ha. Ha. Everybody is laughing but Mama Bones. Even her nephew Gianni smiles, the mamaluke. Lindsay talking this way means Mama Bones and Gianni are history. "I'm serious," Mama Bones says. "It smells so bad, I'm gonna get sick. You better pull over."

That shuts down their jokes.

"You puke in our car," Davenport says. "I'll bust your teeth. Now shut up. We'll be there in five minutes."

Gianni gets Mama Bones attention, slowly wags his head. He smells murder, too. "The Prosecutor's Office is over half an hour from here," he says.

Still on Highway 497, but farther west, less than a mile from Bluefish's, Luis and I hit a traffic jam. We're more than a dozen vehicles behind a roadblock, two police cars perched nose-to-nose with their flashing lights on, plugging the two-lane in both directions. Ahead of us, a column of smoke marks the Bluefish property. That I went on this motorcycle ride with Luis may have saved my life. That I'm still alive ten minutes after handing him the weapon makes me think I was right trusting him once more.

Two pick-ups and a camper swing off the highway ahead of us, battling each other for U-turn space. Trucks and cars behind us do the same thing, and within minutes, a line of stern-faced drivers crawls the opposite way. Since the cops don't mind everyone fleeing, they can't be looking for anybody. Probably keeping gawkers away from the fire.

Luis closes his cellphone. "Mama Bones' number rings but there is still no answer. Perhaps she is unable to hear."

"Or she lost her phone in the fire. Do you have Gianni's number?"

"No. Do you?"

I shake my head. "I can try Emma again."

I listen to the redhead's ring tone. We haven't been able to reach anybody there in well over an hour. "Listen, Luis. I have to ask you something. What's the connection with you and Mama Bones? I know it has something to do with children, but you've always kept it secret."

I hang up when I get Emma's voicemail. I'd rather listen to Luis. My favorite bartender shifts his gaze to stare inside the pine forest on our right, and I realize the semiautomatic rests in his right hand. His thumb works the safety, on and off, on and off.

"There has been no reason for you to know of my business with the Bonacellis," he says. "Nor do I see a reason now."

Funny thing about guns. I believe now Luis is on my

side. He wasn't really going to trade me to the Turk. His thumb isn't working that safety because he's thinking about shooting me. Yet looking at that semiautomatic, remembering the weight of it in my hand, knowing what it can do to human flesh...

"Maybe it's enough for me to know there *is* a connection," I say, "a reason why you'd risk your life and kill for Mama Bones."

Luis glances at the gun and clicks on the safety, then snaps his head up to glare at me. His forehead pinches, an act of raw emotion for the cool Senor Guerrero. "Mama Bones has not been the only beneficiary of my actions."

Oops. Mentally, I run down the checklist: Luis and his wife got me away from the cops at the hospital, saved my life by escaping the bad guys on the Parkway and rescued me again early this morning by tossing a chisel into a man's neck a split second before the bastard shot me.

"Of course," I say. "I'm sorry you think I have forgotten. I owe you my life, Luis many times over. But tonight I worried you had given me to the Turk, or even planned to kill me yourself. I worried because I don't understand what hold Mama Bones has over you."

Luis slips the gun into his jacket. "Our friendship has suffered a difficult night."

A soft, early morning wind carries the smell of burning wood. The brown and green colors of the forest seem unusually vivid. Luis hands me a picture from his wallet. "Here is the reason Mama Bones and I share business and a friendship."

It's an old photograph of teenagers, different ages, but all in khakis and white shirts. They're posed on the steps of what looks like a poor and dirty stone church. Judging by the familiar, handsome teenage face in the last row, I guess the photo to be twenty or twenty-five years old.

"This is you in the back?" I ask.

"*Si*. And Rosalinda in the front row."

I spot Luis' sister now. "A school picture?"

"Not a school. An orphanage administered by the church."

My mouth opens to ask what happened to his parents, but Luis cuts me off. "Because of Mama Bones, St. Theresa's church in Branchtown has what Father Ignacio calls a long-term affiliation with the orphanage where Rosalinda and I were raised."

"I had no idea," I say. "I know Mama Bones is trying to protect some girls who were on their way to Atlantic City. I kind of helped. But I didn't understand to what extent she was involved in aiding children. Thank you for explaining. I understand how personal this is."

Luis shifts his gaze toward the roadblock.

"But I needed to know," I say.

Luis' ancient eyes narrow on something new, and I twist my head to see what captured his attention. The two police cars are pulling apart. They're letting a car from the other side pass through, coming our way through the blockade.

"I wonder if you do understand, *mi amigo*," Luis says. He still watches the roadblock. "It is true that Mama Bones asked for my help with the Turk, but I would not have agreed were *your* life not at risk."

My fist gently punches his shoulder.

"Mama Bones believed there was a chance the Turk would live up to his word and meet me," Luis says. "My plan was to kill him with a weapon belonging to his guards, or if necessary, my bare hands."

"I get it, Luis, but hold that thought—that white Chevy coming through the roadblock and headed toward us—are you watching? I think it's an unmarked police car. I saw one just like it parked illegally at the hospital emergency room yesterday."

Luis motions for me to help him move the motorcycle. "I understand. If the car indeed belongs to Lieutenants Davenport and Lindsay, we do not want them to see us."

"No, we don't."

Luis and I push the motorcycle behind a thick patch of roadside weeds. The unmarked cop car is fifty feet away. "And yet," Luis says, "there are two prisoners in the back of that car. It would be helpful to see who these policemen have arrested, would it not?"

Luis runs back and crouches near the road. I kneel beside the bike and the trees, my back toward the highway and the approaching white Chevy. Its tires hiss on the pavement behind me.

"The car indeed belongs to Lieutenants Davenport and Lindsay," Luis says. "In the back are Mama Bones and Gianni."

The two cops glance at each other and ice cubes dance along Mama Bones' spine. Gianni's shoe starts tapping on the floorboard.

"There's a place to pull over five minutes from here," Davenport says. "A little package goods joint and deli. I want some coffee."

These two crooked cops can do anything they want. They said nothing to nobody back at the lodge, just stuffed her and Gianni in the back seat of their smelly car. Back at their headquarters or the prosecutor's office hours from now, they could say anything happened to their former prisoners. Even something like, *what* former prisoners?

Two miles later, Lindsay slows and veers off the highway into a strip mall. There's an Exxon gas station on the corner. Dust kicks up around the Chevy's back windows. Mama Bones stomach is really acting up.

"Oh boy," she says. "There's a restroom."

Lindsay drives past the gas station, food market and liquor store, turns alongside the strip-mall onto a gravel road that disappears into the pine forest.

"Hey," Mama Bones says. "I'm sick. You gotta let me out of the car."

"We'll be there in a second," Lindsay says. "At my buddy's trailer. I just remembered it's right down this road. Why pay for my coffee?"

Gianni taps Mama Bones on the ankle. She shrugs. What are they gonna do handcuffed in the back seat of a police car?

The Chevy slows and lumbers over tree roots to reach a dirt clearing surrounded by a real forest, not just scrawny pines. An aluminum trailer with rust for window trim rests on one side of the oblong opening, the twenty-foot metal box stuck up on cement blocks.

Lindsay stops the car near the trailer's wooden steps. The bird-faced witch Davenport scrambles out and opens the back door, points her pistol at Mama Bones, say, "Get out."

Mama Bones throws her feet onto the pine needles outside. "So who's this hermit friend of Lindsay's, hide out in this piece of crap, huh?"

"See for yourself," Davenport says.

The trailer's screen door squeaks open. A very big and familiar man steps down into the spackled sunlight. Fat Johnny the Turk Korsay.

* * *

Luis handles the tail-job cool, hanging back at least a quarter mile, adding even more distance on the straightaways. I point out the strip mall as we come around a curve, the white Chevy four-door cruising through an Exxon station on the corner.

Luis pulls over. From a shady spot tucked up against the edge of the weedy pine forest, we watch the Chevy disappear behind the long, one-story building, a huge flock of black birds taking off above the car. We stay put while a black and white cruiser races by on the opposite side of the highway, the cop heading toward the fire scene.

"Where do you think those detectives are taking them?" I ask.

"A place where they can be shot and buried without witnesses."

"Jesus. Are you sure?"

"There could be another explanation," Luis says, "but at the moment I cannot think of one."

"Mama Bones said Davenport and Lindsay were on her payroll as well as the Turk's. Maybe they're going to let Mama Bones and Gianni go."

"I believe it more likely they plan to complete the assassination Turk failed to accomplish last night." Luis throttles up the motorcycle. "We must hurry."

Rocks spew from behind as we swerve through a corner of the strip mall's parking lot. A woman with two small children frowns at us from the shady entrance of a hair and nail salon.

My lips move at her. *Sorry.*

FOURTEEN

The Chevy brakes in a forest clearing one minute later, and Luis swings us into the weeds at the side of the gravel road. He shuts off the motorcycle, but I keep humming. My hands tremble. Maybe it's the motorcycle, maybe it's my recent realization: if Mama Bones and Gianni are killed, I'm a goner, too. Scarier, the Turk's catch-up with Austin Carr could come when I'm tending Elizabeth and Ryan. Both my kids still spend one or two weekends a month with me.

Luis hides the motorcycle deeper inside the forest while I check out the clearing. The cops' Chevy is parked near a thirty-foot, silver-skinned house trailer. I don't see Mama Bones, but Gianni, Davenport and Lindsay walk toward the far side of the clearing and a battered old wooden shed. A mixed forest grows close on all sides. Maples, oaks and locust trees mix with the predominant, scrawny pines. Only the chattering of birds and squirrels breaks the silence.

"What's the plan?" I ask.

Luis gives me the semiautomatic. "You will find cover close to the trailer's entrance. Mama Bones must be inside. I will follow Gianni to the shed. Depending on what I find, and what I can or cannot accomplish, I will come back here, or perhaps cause a distraction. When the two detectives are close, you must shoot them. Be ready in five minutes."

Luis grabs my shoulder. His grip is strong, but he holds my attention with an energy flowing through his long, athletic fingers. He *wills* me to listen. "These two police officers are gangsters. If they are about to murder

Mama Bones and Gianni, are you prepared to kill them instead? Prepared to shoot them in the back?"

I stare at the nine-millimeter in my hand. Kill two cops? Like a husband at home waiting up for his late wife, I worry and wonder.

Mama Bones smiles at Turk's threatening glare. Oh, sure, he's a big shot now, capo of his own little Branch-town family. Calls himself the Turk, but for her, he'll always be that Fat Johnny in school eating two sand-wiches at lunchtime; Fat Johnny at the merry-go-round, too chubby for horses, has to ride the alligator. If her hands weren't tied behind her back, she'd kick his ass and find Gianni.

She might kick Turk's ass anyway. "So you didn't meet with Luis?" she says. "Even though you gave me your word."

"I should have," Turk says. "I'm told your man Luis actually showed up with Carr. I never thought he would. If I'd been there, maybe my boys would have handled it better, killed them both."

"Luis makes a deal, he keeps his word."

"But I don't need to make deals, do I?" Turk says. "I have you, Angelina."

His voice gives her the creeps. "I'm honored you came all the way here to kill me yourself," she says. "Must be some kind of payback for all the times I called you Fat Johnny in school, huh?"

"Probably." He licks his thick lips. "If this happened between us forty years ago, Angelina, I might have tied you to the bed and banged you for a few days. You were hot stuff in high school. Too good for me. It would have been fun to screw your brains out."

Turk scaring her with this rape talk, that mean and

ugly glint in his eyeballs, the nasty one she always saw was there. She says, "Forty years ago, I would have killed you while you tried to tie my hands."

Turk laughs while he opens the little white refrigerator and starts to make himself a corned beef sandwich. The fridge is loaded with the cold cuts. There are enough mustard and mayo jars to open a New York deli.

"So here's the deal," he says. He spreads *Grey Poupon* on two slices of rye bread. "I didn't bring you here to kill you. I want to negotiate, bring an end to this expensive war. All you have to do is give me Austin Carr."

Mama Bones tests the tape around her wrists. Solid. A tight wrap that holds her arms behind her and pins her shoulders rigid against the straight-back chair. She hopes Gianni is still alive. She hasn't seen him in ten minutes. Tomas she hasn't seen or talked to in hours. Since before the explosions.

She says, "Why you want that smarty pants stockbroker so much, huh? He can't hurt you."

Turk uses a ten-inch butcher knife to chop his corned beef sandwich in half. Gobs of yellow mustard ooze from underneath the bread. "No, you're wrong," he says. "That asshole Carr could ruin me."

What I decide, there's no use choosing a location for its access to an easy getaway. If I have to shoot at armed, trained professionals—which these two county cops most definitely are—there's no escape if I miss. Best I choose a hiding place where my inexperienced aim is offered advantage.

Like, close.

That's why ascending this locust tree seemed like a

good idea. Proximity to target. I can't be more than forty feet from the trailer steps, but inside millions of tiny green leaves, stripped of my shirt, I'm practically invisible. I even have a window to shoot through, a thick limb bending under my weight to perfectly display the clearing in front of the trailer.

I'm good as long as no one directly below looks up.

In answer to Luis' question, am I willing to shoot two gangster cops, I say yes, although for me it's important to attach the word gangster. American cities would be unlivable chaos without the police. And it must be among the toughest, most self-sacrificing of jobs. But I'm with Mama Bones in this fight. I have to be. Everything I love rests on what happens here. If I run away and Mama Bones dies, the Turk will eventually come get me. Mama Bones, Gianni and Luis would not only die, this male-female team of crooked Seaside County investigators—or people like them—will find and kill me, too. And how can I live with the chance these gangsters might put a bomb in my car on a day I pick up my kids?

Mama Bones stares at Turk, his chin shiny with corn beef grease. Makes her want to laugh. But her old high school punching bag is serious when he says he wants an answer.

"Why you pointing the gun at me, huh? I heard what you said."

"I want you to understand I'm not kidding," Turk says. "Give me your word you'll bring me Austin Carr, or I'm going to kill you right now, Angelina."

"That's nuts. Of course I'm going to say yes. Sure. I'll bring you the smarty pants stockbroker. What else would anybody say, huh?"

"I said give me your word."

He calls himself the Turk now, like he was some kind of foreigner. But Fat Johnny grew up in Asbury Park, finally thinning out after high school, getting a job cheating the tourists for twelve or fourteen hours during summer days, then dancing to Hank Ballard and Chuck Berry on the radio all night like the rest of them.

"What you think Austin saw, huh?" Mama Bones says.

"None of your business. Give me your word."

"What if he don't even know he saw whatever it was? How do you know he saw it? Did you ask him?"

Turk slips the gun into his coat pocket and picks up the butcher knife, the one with mustard all over it. He runs his thumb across the edge as he walks behind her, then wipes mustard on her black dress, Mama Bones still taped to the chair. Nausea grabs her stomach. What is he going to do with that knife? Mother Mary. Cold steel chills the skin on her wrists, and then her hands come free. He cut her loose. Mama Bones' arms fall forward, numb from the elbows down.

"Stand up," he says.

Mama Bones breathes deeply, slowly through her nose. "Gimme a second, Turk. I'm not in as good shape as you."

He snorts like a pig. "Stop trying to butter me up. I've known you sixty years, Angelina. I know all your tricks. Now stand up and walk outside. Let's see if you're so weak and stubborn when I point the gun at your nephew."

"Okay, okay. I give you my word."

"You give me your word you'll hand over Austin Carr?"

"Yes. I give you my word I'm gonna catch Austin Carr for you. Turn him over to you. Is Gianni okay?

Those two cops didn't hurt him, did they?"

"He was fine the last time I saw him. Why don't we go check? Come on, get on your feet."

Her forearms tingle now, a million dancing needles. That's better than numb. Mama Bones leans forward, hands on the chair for an extra boost. She pretends to wobble onto her feet. "How come I have to go outside after we make a deal, huh? Give me an hour to rest. Then I'll go find Austin."

He shows her the knife. "No, come on, Angelina. I have something to show you."

My body loses tension when Mama Bones shuffles from the trailer. I worried she might be dead already, and the sight of her on the trailer stairs sparks relief, even hope. Mama Bones is not only alive, she's still kicking. A formidable ally. But all my muscle fibers ratchet back tight when I see the Turk swagger out behind her. Where the hell did he come from?

If the Turk hasn't killed her already, maybe the bad cops brought Mama Bones and Gianni here for a face-to-face meeting. Peace negotiations. It's all too much for me. Too complicated. It sure would be nice if I didn't have to shoot anybody.

Mama Bones and the Turk stand side-by-side between the white Chevy and the trailer, in the open. Air hisses between my teeth when I see a semiautomatic in the Turk's right hand. My hopes for a nonviolent day dwindle.

Voices shift my gaze. It's Lieutenants Davenport and Lindsay, shuffling toward Mama Bones and the Turk and pushing something across the clearing. I'm one floor up and see everything.

Lindsay pushes a green, two-wheeled garden carryall,

your basic deep-bucket, high-tech wheelbarrow. The thing squeaks like a wounded animal. Must be a heavy load inside.

Through my hole in the locust leaves, I watch Mama Bones become curious about the two county cops and the big carryall. I can't see what's inside the wheelbarrow yet—the hawk-faced Davenport blocks my view—nor can I hear what the Turk whispers in Mama Bones' ear as his personal police force approaches. Her face shows nothing.

Ten, fifteen feet from the wheelbarrow, close enough to get a good look at its contents, I see Mama Bones' neck and shoulders stiffen. She staggers forward—one, two, three steps closer, focusing on what's inside the green plastic carryall. Her jaw slackens and falls. Her legs buckle.

What is it?

Mama Bones drops to her knees, hands catching herself on the rim of the wheelbarrow. My own heart contracts as if stepped on. What is it? Mama Bones let's go of the carryall and clasps her hands in a prayer.

"Tomas!"

Her voice is a wail that startles the forest. Twenty crows scramble from a seventy-five-foot oak shading Turk's trailer. I want to fly away myself when Davenport shifts and I finally see inside the carryall. I make out enough familiar pieces to recognize Tomas. A shirt, a tattooed arm, most of his burned face.

The Turk pushes against Mama Bones, his knee pressing into her shoulder. "One of the rockets must have exploded pretty close to him," he says.

If the gun in Turk's hand makes peace talks doubtful, Tomas' body and the way Turk rubs Mama Bones' face in it leave no chance this meeting is friendly. I'm betting Luis will make the same decision soon.

I bring my right hand up to join my left in gripping the nine millimeter Luis gave me. I aim the front gun sight at the Turk's chest, although I'll keep my finger off the trigger until I'm ready to fire. I take deep breaths, trying to rein in my galloping heart. Waiting for Luis.

Turk bends over Mama Bones. He's really sticking it to her. "I wanted you to have the body. You don't want the police keeping him for days...the boy will get ripe, if you know what I mean."

Mama Bones pushes off her knees and onto her feet. She pivots away from Davenport, Lindsay and the wheelbarrow to face the Turk. Her neck muscles flex like straining steel wires. I can't see the look she gives him. I can only imagine.

Turk says, "I need to make a point with you, Angelina...remind you what I can and will do if you decide not to bring me Austin Carr."

Oh, hell. I *am* the prize in this war.

Mama Bones can't talk. But her right foot drags forward.

"You and Gianni can take Tomas home," Turk says. "Lieutenants Davenport and Lindsay will drive you. But I expect you to deliver Carr to me by dinner tomorrow. Bring him here."

Mama Bones' spine goes stiff. Her fingers ball into fists. The shuffle toward the Turk is slow, zombie-like. The sparks don't fly visibly. You have to know her. But there's a fuse burning on Mama Bones' neck.

Time to leave. No use risking someone will see me, not if the Turk's going to let Mama Bones and Gianni go. That's why I haven't heard from Luis.

On my perfectly bent tree branch, I slide back a few inches. A loud *crack* vibrates through me, head to tail. The limb I'm on snaps and drops three feet. I lose my grip and fall into the clearing.

FIFTEEN

Mama Bones never understood what it meant, seeing red. She's been angry, ranting and raving, spitting mad. But even the night she killed that robber who shot her Domenic, or the time she smacked her husband over the head with a new lamp he didn't like, she never saw any colors. Not before today, anyway. Now she knows. The Turk is smeared in her vision by cherry-red goo—a bloody film of hate. Tomas' blood. She could rip the skin off Turk's ugly face with her fingers.

She breathes through her nose, her jaws are so tight. Turk made a big mistake showing her Tomas' body in that wheelbarrow, her nephew broken and crushed like some poor animal run over in the street. If she lives to be two hundred years old, Mama Bones will never forget what Turk did to her sister's youngest boy. Never.

And now Turk makes an even bigger mistake. He underestimates his old high school classmate by twisting away from Mama Bones to check Smarty Pants falling out of the tree. Sure, it's pretty crazy Austin Carr tumbling from the sky like that, but Mama Bones is so angry, so focused on pummeling Turk, all she can think, what a perfect diversion.

"Look who dropped in," Turk says. "I can't believe how fast you delivered on your promise, Angel—"

Mama Bones was hopping sideways, lining up the perfect angle, soon as Turk started talking. Thus positioned directly behind him, she kicks Turk as hard as she can between the legs when he calls her name, making sure to crush his testicles with her ankle, not the sneaker on her foot.

Turk doubles over, the son-of-a-bitch groaning high-pitched, like the pig he is, and Mama Bones reaches inside his coat, grabs the gun, the weapon sliding out of his pocket easily from behind. Using Turk for cover, she checks the safety while stepping to the side, extending the gun away from her chest with both hands. Davenport's drawing her weapon, so it's the woman-cop Mama Bones shoots first.

The noise and the recoil wobble her knees. Her body is sore and her muscles tired. But Davenport has a red stain on her chest, and the beak-faced cop's eyes are as big and blank as doorknobs.

Mama Bones slides the gun sight onto a crouching Lindsay. The freckled face cop has his weapon out of the brown leather holster, but not all the way. He's not ready to shoot. Surprised maybe Mama Bones dropped his partner.

Mama Bones fires twice at his chest. The bullets stand Lindsay upright and hold him there. The semiautomatic spills from his hand, the weapon skidding across the pine needles, twisting slowly. His knees buckle. He doesn't—

Turk's fist slams into Mama Bones' hands, knocking the gun from her grip. She forgot about Turk. It's a bad mistake. The gun flies away like a wild bird.

Turk stiff-arms her in the chest, crushing her right breast. Mama Bones yelps with pain and staggers backward to escape the pressure. He punch-pushes again, and she can't keep her balance. She stumbles, her bottom crashing on the clearing's hardpan.

She rolls onto her shoulder, then her belly, trying to remember where she is in relation to Turk's gun. The noise and adrenaline make things confusing. She shot, maybe killed, two cops.

She pushes up on her hands and knees. Pine needles dangle from her hair onto her cheeks. Where is that gun?

The Turk is gonna find it first and kill her any second.

There it is. Five feet away.

She scrambles on all fours then dives on her belly, her right arm stretching for the semiautomatic. Reaching for her life.

Turk steps on her wrist. She gasps as pain shoots up her arm.

"You crazy bitch," he says. "I should have killed you as soon as I took over for Bluefish."

He snatches his semiautomatic off the pine needles and straightens to his full six-foot-five height, Turk towering above her. His lips spread into a smile as he aims the gun at her little pug nose, the one Domenic used to call a button.

Another gunshot thunders, blood exploding from Turk's throat at the same instant, Turk losing any last minute words and a chunk of his neck.

Blood swamps the Turk's chest. He pitches forward.

Mama Bones rolls out of the way so Fat Johnny don't fall on top of her, but she feels his sticky blood splash onto her cheek and into her hair.

Mother Mary. Her stomach rolls and flips like a puppy.

I'm not sure what surprises me more, Mama Bones pulling off the Wyatt Earp imitation, blasting two gunslingers in two seconds, or me doing my Robert Ford parody, Ford being the guy who shot Jesse James in the back. I didn't lose Luis' weapon when I fell out of the tree, and I only considered a split second asking Turk to drop his gun, raise his hands. I saw what happened. Turk was pulling the trigger on Mama Bones.

How many days ago was it I came back from vacation determined to quit the business; absolutely resolved to leave all co-employment with people named Bonacelli? What happened? As I ponder, my ears still ring from the gunfire, especially my own blast that took out Turk's neck. I killed somebody.

The forest is dead quiet but for the echoes of death. There is a sense of unreality surrounding me like a blanket, but I throw it off and walk over beside Mama Bones. "Are you all right?"

"I'll live," she says. She uses my hand to pull herself up.

Shoes run on the pine needles and dirt behind me. Mama Bones smiles. It's Luis and Gianni, jogging toward us from the shed. Luis' boots track a path between faint marks left by the wheelbarrow.

"What the hell happened?" Gianni says.

"Your brother is dead," Mama Bones says.

Gianni nods. "I saw Tomas in the shed. Who killed Davenport and Lind—"

"I shot those two killer cops," Mama Bones says. She wipes her nose. "Smarty Pants had to take out the Turk."

"Mama Bones looked like Wild Bill Hickok," I say. "Kicked Turk in the balls, took his gun and shot Davenport and Lindsay before they could draw."

Luis checks out the broken tree branch. "You fell from the tree?"

An hour later, Mama Bones touches my arm in the back row of a Chevy Suburban belonging to Gianni's friend, Tommy Tunes. Luis drove his motorcycle home, and Tommy's taking the rest of us back to Branchtown. "Turk says you saw something at the racetrack that night that could hurt him, ruin his deal," she says. "Have you figured out what it was yet?"

"I can't imagine."

"Maybe it doesn't matter anymore," Mama Bones says. "Turk's dead. Whatever he was planning at the track is maybe finished, too."

"I have no clue," I say.

Gianni and I searched Turk's trailer and the trunk of the cops' Chevy. We found files and a lock-box containing check-stubs and corporate ownership documents linking Turk, Lindsay and Davenport in a pay-day lending business, proof, Gianni says, that only "dirty cops get their asses shot." We did some cleaning, left three bodies in the clearing, Turk's weapon and the documents on the front seat of the Chevy. Tomas came with us.

"There is no way in hell Turk planned on robbing the track," Gianni says. "Fifty guys and a M1 Abrams tank couldn't do it."

"Okay, so it's a cover story," Mama Bones says. "What other big scores are there at the racetrack?"

"There was nothing in Turk's trailer," Gianni says. "Not a hint."

"How about every horse bettor's prayer?" I say. "Cashing in the only winning ticket."

Mama Bones says goodnight to Big Frank in New York, clicks off her cell phone as Gianni rests a mug of steaming hot cocoa on her night stand. She can't remember the last time she went to bed at six o'clock on a summer evening. Maybe the day her daughter was born.

"You heard the end of that conversation?" Mama Bones asks. "Maybe some of Frank screaming back?"

Gianni nods.

"It went pretty good, right?"

"Okay. Frank didn't sound that mad," Gianni says. "But you can't tell with him on the phone. We'll know how Frank and the rest of New York feels when we see them tomorrow."

"Let's take the boat, huh? The weather's supposed to be good."

"If you want." Gianni stops halfway out of her bedroom. "I don't see how New York can be that mad at you. Turk's the one who shot rockets from a helicopter, got all the TV coverage."

"The news I saw, they called it a Fourth of July prank." Mama Bones sits on the edge of her bed and lifts the hot chocolate to her lips. Too hot. "I'm not so worried about New York. Frank was trying to sound mad, which means he wasn't. And little girl sex slaves is a thing none of them want to read about. But I'm missing some connection with the racetrack."

"I don't understand," Gianni says.

"I'm supposed to be in charge now—at least temporarily—but I don't know what was supposed to happen, or what's going to happen at the track this weekend."

Gianni shrugs. "Maybe the whole story's a load of crap."

"You think? But why did Turk kill Heriberto Garzia? And what else did Austin see? Turk told me it could ruin him."

Gianni shakes his head. "I don't know, and I'm too tired to care."

The doorbell wakes me from a dream about shooting the Turk. I slept so hard, it takes me four or five seconds to figure out where I'm at—home, alone and exhausted.

I answer in my sweat bottoms, each step producing

pain from activities of the previous twenty-four hours. My shoulder's the worst—where Turk's bullet took a piece of me, but my hip hurts from falling out of the tree, and my chin where Luis nailed me feels like a bus smacked it.

I open the front door for Emma Tierney. She rolls into my condo like the cherry bomb I met that first night at Taki's, smoking hot in a crimson sweater, tight jeans and a halo of red hair spun gold by the yellow porch light behind her. I smell gardenias in her wake. All my pains subside.

"I thought you'd be happy to see me," the redhead says. She surveys the living room, her back to me. "Weren't you worried I got blown up by those Fourth of July rockets? I heard about the lodge burning on the radio."

She didn't come here to talk about last night.

I close the door behind us and slide my hands around her waist. She gazes back at me, excitement thick in her blue eyes. "Mama Bones told me you left right after Luis and I took off on the motorcycle," I say. "She wondered if maybe you knew the Turk was going to attack."

"No, that's not true," she says. "Once you and Luis left, I didn't feel safe. I wanted to be where no one could find me."

She spins out of my hands. "Do you have anything alcoholic to drink?"

Like a trout chasing a lure, I follow the redhead into my kitchen. Her gardenia perfume hangs thick along the trail, and I make the entire journey without taking my eyes off her rear end. Emma's jeans fit her like paint.

"I have wine and beer, a little tequila," I say.

Emma spins and leans against me, her hands on my cheeks. She raises onto her toes to kiss me. The soft, womanly press of her takes physical custody of me. I am enveloped in a flowery fog, her mouth melting against mine like warm sweet chocolate.

Making me want it all.

We embrace and my right hand slides down the curve of her hip, gently urging her against me. She squeezes me back tighter.

I think Emma and I are about to make love.

SIXTEEN

Saturday afternoon, Gianni wants to stay downstairs at the bar and drink, so Mama Bones has to poke and prod ten minutes before he escorts her up to the ferry boat's top deck. Three flights of steel stairs on her sore back, Mama Bones needs a nephew's help. And now only one is all she has.

It's beautiful weather on top, even Gianni admits, the sun getting low but still shining, the air warm but not hot, the ocean wind cooling her skin. The smells of the summer are strong up here; memories of a lifetime growing up on the Jersey Shore. They didn't wear bikinis in her high school days, but Mama Bones had a figure the boys wanted look at and talk about.

"I'm glad we took the boat, huh?" she says.

Gianni nods. "Less hassle than driving, for sure. How's your back after those stairs?"

"I'm fine. How's your knee?"

He shakes his head, a smile on his face. "So how does it feel to be capo, the first female boss of Seaside County? Maybe any Jersey county."

Mama Bones clutches Gianni's arm, tugs him as far forward as ferry passengers are allowed. Not quite the bow. The wind is stronger, pulling strands of hair from her tortoise-shell clips, snapping her black dress. No one could ever hear them talking. "Not so hot," she says.

"What's not to like? Your income should double. And we don't have to worry any more about the Turk putting the squeeze on us about the women you help."

"No, now we gotta worry about Turk's crew—those guys who don't want to work for a woman, think I'm weak."

Gianni shakes his head. "Everybody knows you, knows you're fair, that you've always spread the wealth. That's what our thing is down here, business. Everybody knows your family has been part of this for a century."

"They don't think I'm a silly old woman?"

"Not one guy, especially after what happened in the Pine Barrens. Taking away the Turk's gun and shooting two cops with it? Mama Bones, nobody—and I mean nobody—thinks you're weak or silly."

She grunts. She was mad, that's all.

"You're a Jersey Shore legend," he adds.

Her improved sense of well-being, brought on by warm sunlight and salty fresh air, vanishes. Whatever she is or will be, for whatever time she has left on this earth, she no longer has Tomas. No matter how much work she does through St. Theresa's, no matter how much money she earns as boss, her nephew is never coming back. She'd trade everything to have Tomas.

Gianni drives them out of the Highlands ferry parking lot in silence, and Mama Bones decides to push from her thoughts the sadness over Tomas. Not to mention her glory days, those teenage summer nights, after work on the beach. If she's going to be capo, she better start taking care of business.

Waiting for the light at Highway 36, she says, "I have to know what Turk had up his sleeve about that horse track."

Gianni snorts.

"You know what I mean," she says. "Why you gotta laugh? You can't do that around other people no more."

"Yes, ma'am."

"Good. I've changed my mind about where we're going, too. Drop me off at the library on Highway 35 before you head to the track."

"What's at the library?"

"Old newspapers. I want to read everything I can about Croc Tierney, our indicted and fugitive ex-mayor. I might remember stuff."

Something Smarty Pants said yesterday had Mama Bones thinking about Croc Tierney all last night.

"Croc Tierney is ancient history," Gianni says.

"I gotta hunch. Remember how Croc used to love the ponies?"

"No."

"Well, that's what Croc always talked about, what he spent all his bribe money on. The Gambling Mayor is what the newspapers called him."

"So?"

"So Emma Tierney said at my house that night she might be seeing her father. She said Croc Tierney was in town to visit Turk, maybe get his money back."

"I remember Emma saying that, but what does Croc have to do with Turk's big deal at the track?"

"That's the hunch part, sure," Mama Bones says. "The connection. But since the Feds are still searching for our ex-mayor, it's gotta be a real important reason for Croc to come back here, a place where people would recognize him. Remember what Smarty Pants said in the car yesterday? Austin's gotta a nose for money he don't even know about."

"What did he say?"

"That all you need to score big at the racetrack is one winning ticket."

"A winning ticket?" Gianni says. "You think the Turk fixed a race—is that what you're saying? But the

Turk doesn't have a horse running this weekend."

"You sure? That kills the idea. But I still want to read those stories again and do some research on horse racing."

"If you take the ex-mayor's picture from the library, I could have our linen guys call all their hotels and motels, ask if they've seen him."

"If Croc's in town, I don't think he'll be staying in a motel. He's too smart to stay at his sister's, too. If he's in town to see the Turk, pretty sure he goes for Turk's compound. It's what his daughter Emma kinda hinted at."

"Who's Croc's sister again?" Gianni asks.

"Barbara Ryder."

I turn into a quarter-mile circular driveway lined on both sides by five-story conifers, mostly pine and cypress. Heavily shaded this late in the day, and with a damp smell from the nearby river, this long approach to Barbara Ryder's house makes her three-story, tile roofed villa appear dark and foreboding. Emma and I carried towels and coffee down to the shore to watch the sunrise early this morning, ended up swimming in our underwear, then dressing and eating a full breakfast at the Pardon Me Diner. When I dropped her off here afterward, we made a date for dinner, and now—rested, showered, shaved and caught up with my two kids—I'm pulling into Barbara Ryder's Rumson estate for the second time in nine hours. Loose gravel squishes and pops beneath the tires as I brake my Solara at the front steps.

Emma and I enjoyed a fantastic morning. Lots of laughs. Warm friendship. Like me, she enjoys baseball, runs her own fantasy team. I couldn't believe the way she spouted off about pitchers, how she says it's so important in weekly leagues to keep a long reliever or two. I could see myself falling for her, even though I don't really want a relationship. I find myself thinking of Patricia Willis a lot, the redhead who disappeared after we shared love and insider trading charges last fall. But even forgetting my feelings for Patricia, seriously dating Emma wouldn't be fair—or healthy for her. Over the course of a four-decade lifetime, I'm zero for seven with redheads: if you don't count Margie Fleming in the seventh grade, every one of my beloved red-haired lovers is now dead or in prison. Bullets usually, although I remember one who got tossed in the Atlantic Ocean forty miles from land. Kelly, her name was.

I've heard it said women need to fall in love in order to have sex, while men need sex in order to fall in love. Now this axiom could be pure baloney for most guys, but it speaks directly to me. I have to be careful. Experience has taught me cruel lessons. And while Emma definitely stirs my passions—that is, I sense the sex working on my tender heart—there is something sad in her eyes that bothers me. Sad isn't right.

Probably something I don't understand.

I cut the engine and climb outside. Ryder's landscaping reminds me of a medical building, particularly the extra parking and the over-trimmed foundation plantings. Each four-foot evergreen bush is a perfectly neat lollipop. I happen to know the property. This place runs eighteen acres, on the river, across the street from Bruce Springsteen. The house itself is a thirty-room, U-shaped Italian villa; boxy looking except for the ornate window trimmings and the sloped, clay tile roof. Five chimneys.

My shoes crunch on the rock driveway. The tips of Italian cypress peak above the villa's roof line, probably around the swimming pool I've always imagined to be in the center of the U-shaped building. On the side yard, well-trimmed grass slopes toward the Navasquan River. The view is of hillside estates two miles across the water.

The twelve-foot tall, hand-carved, double front door splits open before I can knock. Emma greets me in cutoff blue jeans, leather work boots and a long-sleeve, plaid flannel shirt. Maybe on our date tonight, Emma the lumberjack wants to chop down trees. My sport coat and slacks begin to itch.

"Barbara wants us to have dinner here," Emma says. "Do you mind?"

"Of course not. I love moose stew."

Emma's smile wrinkles. Two beats. "Oh...my clothes." She laughs. "I was fishing off the boat dock." She pulls me inside an ornately decorated foyer. A rectangular mirror hangs above a marble-topped library table. A three-foot-tall yellow Chinese ginger jar holds a peacock-tail spray of blue and blood-red iris.

"The doctor who owned this house before your aunt used to buy bonds from me," I say, "but I was never invited inside. I always wanted to see the pool."

Emma guides me into a room with stuffed chairs, two sofas and floor-to-ceiling stuffed bookcases. "There's no swimming pool. What are you talking about?"

"All those cypress tree sticking up behind the house. I thought they—"

"They're a wind break for my iris."

Close behind, a newcomer startles me with her interruption—a trim, fifty to sixty-year-old woman in a low-cut, electric blue dress. Her features are sharp, like a bird's, mainly because of the thin nose and round eyes. She stands less than a foot away, pushing into my space. Her proximity is uncomfortable and I can't hide it.

She offers me her hand. "Mr. Carr, I presume. I'm Barbara Ryder, Emma's aunt."

The medicinal taste of vodka haunts her breath, and the blue dress with push-up bra is too revealing for a woman her age, seems to me. Obviously, Barbara Ryder doesn't think so. She's thin and tan, so she probably works out five days a week under a sunlamp. But like the dark and damp approach to her house, Emma's aunt fills me with unease. Instinctively, I retreat a step before shaking her hand.

Mama Bones sticks her head back inside Gianni's old Jeep. Smells like dirty gym socks. "Come and get me in an hour, huh? And don't forget, put a watch on Turk's as well as Barbara Ryder's. I hear there's an open house at Turk's place after the viewing. Maybe our ex-mayor Croc Tierney is dumber than we think."

Gianni pulls away, leaving her in the half-full library parking lot. In Mama Bones' high school days, after the summer tourist season was over and you were back in school, the Asbury Park Library was the best place to meet your friends for a night on the town. You'd rent a book early, mess around all night, but stop by the library before 10 p.m. and take out another. You could drink a bottle of vodka, or party with the starting basketball team, your parents believed you were probably studying all night because of the library's official time-stamps.

At the well-hidden information desk, Mama Bones' friend Caldonia glances up from her computer screen, smiles when he sees Mama Bones. "Oh hello, Angelina. How you doing?"

"Pretty good. Not too bad. How's Patsy?"

"Much better, thanks to you. Those men you sent fixed up his house in one week—new walkways, an elevator. It changed my father's life, Angelina. Honestly. It was such a generous thing for you to do."

Mama Bones waves her off. "Those guys with the elevator company owed me a favor. Plus, I told them how much you've done for me and the church women who need help with their English. You gotta know Father Ignacio is very grateful."

"Yes, he called a few weeks ago. But you must let me thank you, Angelina. You are a kind and generous person. Thank you for helping my father."

Mama Bones lets her face flush.

"Now," Caldonia says, "is there something I can help *you* with this evening?"

"Two things. I want to read the *Branchtown Sun's* stories on Steven Tierney, the ex-mayor who got indicted for bribery a few years ago."

"That's easy. I'll show you the special website they have, the microfilm if the stories go back far enough."

"Plus, I want to research different ways people fix horse races."

Caldonia lifts an eyebrow.

SEVENTEEN

Barbara Ryder attaches herself to me as we stride off her brick patio minutes later. Her hand chills my elbow. Her fingers are like ice cubes. We carry our drinks onto the gray stone path of her award-winning flower garden. I know the garden's a prize winner because there's a silver, chalice-shaped plague stuck in the dirt that says so. "Beside my grand prize winning iris," Ryder says, "I'm afraid there's not much else blooming this time of year. The azaleas finished last week and that nasty Hurricane Sandy killed every single one of my rhododendrons."

Emma lingers three steps behind her aunt and me. "That won't stop you from taking us on the two-hour tour," she says. Emma's voice is different than it was this morning or even when I arrived minutes ago. Higher pitched. Stressed. "How about we finish our drinks and sit down for dinner?" Emma says.

Ryder ignores her. "I suppose I should listen to my gardener and re-plant a few rhododendrons. The red ones are quite beautiful."

Nothing indirect about the current between these two. The tension's flowed steadily since I admired the blue and red iris in the foyer's Chinese ginger jar. Ryder seized the opportunity to show me her gardens, and Emma seemed disappointed, now angry. I am not looking forward to breaking bread between the two combatants. Wonder if there's a back door out of here?

"Of course my blue irises are a show in themselves," Ryder says. "I win a Seaside County Fair breeders award every year. Maybe you've seen my name in the paper."

"Probably," I say. "These colors certainly are beautiful."

Emma finishes her scotch. "Irises are the easiest plant in the world to breed." She shakes her ice cubes. "Not like Mrs. Rosalini's orchids."

I sip the Wild Turkey Ryder fixed me. Whatever conflict these two share, the tension is high enough to make me jumpy. I worry that Ryder holds one arm while a bourbon occupies the other. Luis taught me a warrior does not stand or walk with his hands in his pockets, or otherwise occupied.

Why do I feel threatened? They're not mad at me.

"Did you make anything for dinner?" Emma says. "Or are we calling out for Chinese?"

The tone in Emma's voice feels wrong to me, like a child snapping at its mother. Emma acts in a manner exactly opposite the way she behaved with me this morning, that is, mature, self-confident and thoughtful of others. If these two are fighting, why have dinner together—and invite me?

Ryder halts our tour beside a bed of tall blue iris. "This one is called Azure Nights."

"It's gorgeous," I say.

Maybe Emma doesn't like playing second string to the vegetation. She crowds up behind her aunt, so close we have to look, and the expression on Emma's face is pursed and ugly, like she tasted a sour grapefruit. "Austin and I have to go," she says.

That's not a bad idea. At least those are *my* thoughts on the subject. Ryder, not so much. "Oh, I don't think that's possible now, dear."

"The hell it isn't," Emma says.

"Oh, but I've prepared a wonderful roast leg of lamb, with scalloped potatoes and fresh peas. I'm waiting on the roast. Oh, Emma, I've spent hours—"

"Screw your fresh peas," Emma says.

I touch Emma's shoulder and try to hold her gaze. "Are you okay?"

Emma doesn't answer me. The redhead has that blank look in her blue eyes again, as if she turned off inside. It could be fear, but it's hard to say. She doesn't look mad. She seems distracted. Out of touch.

"Besides my own preparations," Ryder says, "you exerted some yourself today. Surely, you remember the cabinet you prepared for him? You don't want to throw that work away, do you?"

What is Ryder talking about? Prepared who? For what?

"Actually, I do want to throw it away," Emma says. Her eyes spark back to life. She grabs my arm. "Let's go, Austin. You can take me out for Mexican."

Ryder shrugs. "As I said, Emma dear, I'm afraid it's too late."

Emma ignores her aunt. In her cutoff jeans and plaid flannel shirt, Emma leads me back toward the brick patio and house. If my date wants to ditch her flower-obsessed aunt, who am I to object? Emma's legs look wonderful in those cutoffs, and there's no way she'll feel uncomfortable at Luis'.

Emma sets a fast pace. My pulse zips higher. Two steps from the brick patio the bourbon and the pounding ticker hit me like a fifty-caliber machine gun bullet. Geez. I'm stopped in my tracks. Dizzy. My toes and fingertips go cold, then numb. The rock steps back to the patio are lighted by stakes in the ground, but now they glow hypnotically. Vaporous.

I stagger forward. My left shoe catches the first brick of the stepped up patio. I trip and sink into a rolling tumble, spilling the drink and shattering Ryder's hand-engraved, crystal cocktail glass. I bang my hip and my elbow, and though I don't feel the pain in my head, I must crack that, too, because I'm on the ground and can't get up. My muscles don't respond to commands. In addition to bourbon and common tap water, did I ingest something else as well—a fifth of absinthe? Magic mushrooms?

Emma bends over me. Gosh I love those freckles. Her auburn hair falls alongside her cheeks. Those strange blue eyes are now the exact color of her aunt Barbara Ryder's prize-winning iris, Azure Nights.

Emma whispers, "Are you okay?"

I can't make a sound.

Feet shuffle up behind my head. Must be Ryder.

Emma glances up. "You poisoned him?"

An hour before the library closes at ten o'clock, Mama Bones touches Caldonia's shoulder on the way out, thanks her for her help. When she finds Gianni in the parking lot, she climbs into his ragtop Jeep, says, "I didn't get any ideas where our ex-mayor might be hiding, but I got a good hunch on what Smarty Pants saw, what Turk could have been planning."

Gianni looks left before turning onto Highway 35.

"You know, at the racetrack?" she says. "Austin thought Turk wanted him dead because Austin saw the murder?"

"Yeah," Gianni says. "And?"

"I think Turk was worried about the little gray horse."

Gianni pulls away from the library, the Jeep leading a pack of traffic north, Gianni's head shaking, no way, no way. "You're making too much of completely separate facts—one, that the ex-mayor might be in town, and two, that Turk maybe had plans for the racetrack. Those two things don't have to be connected."

"Maybe. Do we still have people near Turk's and Ryder's?"

"Yup. Tommy Tunes is actually inside Turk's house at the reception. He's a high school friend of the oldest son's. And so you know, Dustin says your favorite stockbroker is visiting Barbara Ryder, not Croc Tierney."

Mama Bones watches the red tail lights of a furniture delivery truck. Austin must be at Ryder's with that redhead, Emma Tierney. Daughter of the ex-mayor.

"No comment?" Gianni says.

She grunts. "You hungry?"

Mama Bones decides the waitress flirting with Gianni would be a perfect wife for him, a pretty Italian girl with dark hair and creamy skin. Reminds her a little of herself about forty-five years ago. Too bad the only thing Gianni wants to stare at is Cassiota's menu.

"I'll start with a Caesar salad," Gianni says, "if you can hold the anchovies."

The waitress smiles. Nice teeth. Her golden brown eyes sparkle. "For you, sure."

"I love anchovies," Mama Bones says. "My mama used to make sandwiches out of them for my school lunch."

Gianni watches the waitress leave. "So tell me more about this hunch. You think the Turk was going to fix a race tomorrow?"

Mama Bones reaches for her purse. "Maybe he still does. Not him, for sure, but Croc Tierney. I figure the ninth race, right after the Seaside Handicap."

"How's that possible...in today's security-minded world?"

"Jockeys still get bribed or blackmailed. Stewards, too. You know, the guys in those towers with binoc—"

"I know what a steward is," Gianni says.

Mama Bones pulls out a *The Daily Racing Form*. "Okay, the racetrack knows all this, too. They got people who watch the stewards, different people to keep their eye on the jockeys, people who watch the watchers. The best way to cheat, the only way hardly anyone ever gets caught, I read about in *License to Kill*, a post-Ian Fleming James Bond novel."

Gianni's thick eyebrows inched higher, like caterpillars. "Post what?"

"The librarian explained to me," she says.

"Okay, I'll bite. So what's the best way to cheat at horse racing?"

"Twin horses," Mama Bones says. "It's so rare, nobody even looks for it. About one in every ten-thousand deliveries, a mare drops twins. But even rarer than that, one twin is fast and the other is faster. My hunch is Austin saw what no one was supposed to see— a ringer horse. Maybe Zip Your Lip supposedly left the stable a day earlier. But if Austin started talking about seeing the gray filly, said it to the right people, what he saw could blow the fix."

"There's a horse named Zip Your Lip?"

Mama Bones hands Gianni the folded *The Daily Racing Form*. "She's the gray filly from Argentina in the ninth race tomorrow. Look who owns her."

"Ryder?" Gianni says. "Tierney's sister? Wow, and look at this. Did you check out Zip Your Lip's past performance chart? How she only won once before, in New Jersey, but runs middle of the pack all over South America?"

"I read in an old *Newsweek* the FBI figured Steven Tierney could be hiding in Argentina," Mama Bones says. "They breed a lot of horses down there. It's a place not everybody's on the up and up."

Gianni smiles. "Sounds like Jersey. We raise more thoroughbreds here than Kentucky, too. Did you know that?"

"Get out."

"It's true."

EIGHTEEN

I don't know how much times passes, nor am I certain of my location. Voices have whispered nearby me the whole time, but attempts at word recognition only increased the throbbing in my brain.

Eventually, my cheek recognizes the unfamiliar chill of brick, and I realize I'm right where I dropped—on Barbara Ryder's back patio, Ryder being Emma's aunt and sister to the fugitive Croc Tierney. My consciousness flutters to a better state, pain subsides and the whispering voices eventually become sentences. Barbara Ryder and Emma still argue.

"I don't agree," Ryder says. "I think you'll love Argentina. Buenos Aires is a fabulous, exciting city. Vibrant. There's wonderful music and dancing everywhere, laughter all the time."

"Maybe in the part of town where you hang out," Emma says. "Is Argentina where you bought the horses?"

"Thoroughbreds, dear. Not just horses."

"Why would I want to live with someone who always corrects me? Someone who treats me like a child?"

"You *are* my child."

What? I thought Barbara was Emma Tierney's aunt. There's a cold creeping into my ribs and gut—an internal warning that probably woke me up. My body shouts at me to roll over, change the pressure points. Warm up. But I must remain absolutely still and quiet. There may be more information I can learn.

"I'm twenty-seven years old," Emma says. "I need to live my own life. I don't want to do it in Argentina, under your control."

"Supervision, not control."

"What's the difference?"

"I won't tell you what to do every day," Ryder says. "But I will want to be certain you don't fall in with the wrong crowd, or involve yourself in politics, or some kind of misadventure before you can...well, grow to be totally independent."

"Horse shit."

We were looking at blue iris. I was sipping bourbon, a drink Ryder poured. She must have drugged me.

"Such language. Really, dear," Ryder says. "And may I ask you, is having affairs with Mafia dons and Mexican stable boys the kind of unsupervised behavior you plan to indulge in? Because, believe me, you are lucky you were not killed. I cannot let things like that happen again."

"It's none of your business who I screw."

I hear—but don't see—a loud smack. Sounds like Ryder gave Emma a quick back hand knuckle sandwich. Emma whimpers.

I crank my eyes open, the motion sending a jolt through my unhappy central nervous system. A trickle of blood slides from the corner of Emma's mouth. Looks like Ryder enjoys her violence, drugging me and smacking her niece or daughter around. Ryder's cypress trees outline my cockeyed view of the night sky. Stars blink in a dark stripe.

"And this promiscuous clown of a stockbroker," Ryder says, "I wouldn't be surprised if he didn't present you soon with a venereal disease."

Hey, that's slander. I get checked every year.

Emma and her aunt leave the patio, their voices

moving inside the house, enjoying the summer night while keeping an eye on me in that sun room we strolled through on our way to the iris garden.

"What are you going to do with Austin?" Emma says. Her voice is softer than before, no doubt toned down by Ryder's whack.

"I thought we might feed him to the offshore flounder."

I'm not surprised. And like I said, I'm lucky to have woken up from whatever Ryder added to my Wild Turkey. This cold brick against my cheek could be Navasquan River mud. Forty feet beneath the surface. I'm alive, and that means I've got a chance, although I'm guessing it won't be my big mouth that saves me this time. Not with these two.

"Why bother killing him if we're going back to Argentina?" Emma asks.

"Because he saw Zip Your Lip when our money-maker was supposed to be on her way to Buenos Aires."

"You mean the ringer?" Emma asks.

Bells go off in my head, too. A five-alarm fire. Zip Your Lip—that insultingly named, gray filly—is the horse who almost killed me the night Heriberto died. Oh my. This explains a lot. The gray filly was a ringer—a con I thought no longer possible because of today's identifying tattoos and such. I want to jump up and shout, although the info isn't going to do me much good if I'm flounder food.

"Why don't you get our bags and coats," Ryder says. "I'm going to use the potty, then check your stockbroker to see if the sedative is wearing off. It's about time to get on the boat. You are completely packed, I hope."

Boat? And packed for what, I wonder? Argentina's a long way off.

I hear faint steps, but I can only hope they're not

watching as I roll onto my side. My plan is to push up onto my hands and knees, rally from there back onto my feet. If I take a couple of deeps breaths maybe my legs will want to get mobile, my head sharp-witted again. With luck, I could stagger out a side gate and find my Toyota. The keys are in my pocket, poking my thigh.

Turns out I don't feel like standing up. My body would rather go back to sleep. But the will to live is stronger. Right? Come on, Austin. Get up. I know this might be my only chance at survival.

On my hands and knees, I throw up, spilling mainly my chance for stealth. Not much left of that spiked bourbon, but the sound of my retching cuts through the riverside garden night. My vision circles down a slow drain, spinning clockwise into a single square inch of Barbara Ryder's brick walkway. A red and porous world of ants.

I'm not standing up any time soon. But lucky me, I can still think. If both Ryder and the Turk want me dead because of what I saw—well, Turk's estate—then Ryder and the Turk were working together. *Are* working together, except the Turk's dead. I know because I shot him. But Ryder's still working.

Maybe I'm not thinking as well as I thought.

But what I saw, why everybody wants to kill me, is that small gray thoroughbred, Zip Your Lip. I saw her at the track the night Turk killed Heriberto, and someday a good cop will take my statement, know the gray filly could not be in two places at once.

The spinning dizzies subside. I push off the patio with my hands and lean back into a kneeling position, knees rubbing on the brick, butt on my heels. I take a couple of deep breaths. It's chilly by the river. Or maybe lying on this outside walkway for half the evening had a heat-draining effect.

I wish my head would clear. I need to leave. One Florsheim slides up underneath me. I'm ready to stand on my two feet again. Ready to assume the position of a fully conscious, free and independent man.

Oops. Guess not. Before I straighten all the way, a heavy hand pushes on my shoulder, forcing me back down to one knee. The grip is strong.

"Where do you think you're going?" Ryder says.

I glance up. "I was hoping the horse track. I need to make a bet on that small gray filly running tomorrow."

Her thin lips part into a wicked smile. Like the Mona Lisa. Everybody thinks that famous Da Vinci smirk is enigmatic, but the poison has always been obvious to me.

Ryder's fingers feel like pliers when they move to the bandage on my opposite shoulder. She digs her thumb inside my muscle through the wound Turk made with a bullet. I scream in pain.

"The roll of duct tape is on the lamp table in the sun room," Ryder says. "Would you get it for me, Emma dear?"

Mama Bones finishes her dinner, dabs the linen napkin across her lips. "Where did Austin take that redhead Emma Tierney tonight after the aunt's, huh?"

"I don't know," Gianni says. He's been finished with his meal a long time, but only now he searches for the waitress. He cocks his head to the side, showing Mama Bones he could use a haircut. She can't see the top of his ears.

She says, "I thought your guy was going to keep watch on Austin when he left Barbara Ryder's."

"I told my man." To the cute Italian waitress, Gianni makes a writing motion in the air. She nods back like he asked her to marry him. "He's probably still there," Gianni says.

"Why, you think?"

"If he wasn't, I would have heard."

"I mean why would Austin and Croc Tierney's daughter stay at Ryder's? Why wouldn't they want to be alone?"

"I don't know."

"Check with your man."

She tries not to worry watching Gianni use his phone. Turk is gone, but Turk's plan could still be in play, Austin still a threat to someone. No reason in the world Tierney's sister Barbara Ryder couldn't be a part of it.

Gianni punches the phone keys so fast, he reminds Mama Bones of that two-sweaters-a-month knitting lady at the church, and Gianni's head still hangs over the cell when the waitress brings the check. She sticks around, too. Lingering. But Gianni won't look up. He's reading the screen.

Only when the waitress leaves does he glance at Mama Bones. "It's like I said. Austin's still there—at Ryder's. Dustin says it looks like he's going to spend the night. All the house lights are out, the place is quiet."

Mother Mary. She reaches for her purse. "I'm heading for the car while you pay the check. We gotta go look." What did she forget, huh? What mistake did she make now? Something is way wrong over there.

Emma and Ryder roll me onto a double-bed size piece of canvas tarp. They use the dark stained lawn cloth to drag me onto a wheeled handcart like you see in the parking lot of big home improvement stores. People load the carts up with manure and mulch, take the stuff home to throw all over their yard.

Ryder and Emma pull me through a side garden trail onto the estate's dock, my limp body bouncing hard over every brick and rock. I hear a party across the water, a drummer leading the live band. Thump thump. Thump thump. The heart of rock and roll.

"Was that your brother earlier?" I ask. "I heard a man talking."

Our procession stops near a white, chrome-trimmed motor yacht. Clean and new, maybe thirty feet in length.

"I don't have a brother," Ryder says.

Ten minutes later Mama Bones knots the black silk scarf under her chin. It's the same scarf she wore to Domenic's viewing and burial, the one she bought herself in Florence when they went to Italy for their fifth wedding anniversary. She wears it like armor sometimes, and tonight she knows she's being a little reckless, going with Gianni and his men inside Barbara Ryder's Rumson estate. There's a possibility of bullets. But she wants to be there in case this is the big finish. She's pretty sure now that ex-mayor Croc Tierney and his sister Barbara made a deal with Turk, something to do with twin horses and a ringer to race for the ex-mayor's old debts. And it was that deal, their plan, that killed Tomas. And maybe already killed Austin, too.

"I'm going inside with you," she says.

"No way," Gianni says. "If you're right about this, there could be gunfire. Croc Tierney won't want to be caught."

"I been around gunshots. Even fired a few, huh?"

Gianni cuts the Escalade's engine. They're parked a long half block from Barbara Ryder's estate by the river, on a side street. It's dark in these fancy, big money neighborhoods. Rumson—where the trees are two or three times as old as the maples on Mama Bones' Branchtown street. These big trees with a full summer roof of branches and leaves block even the moon and stars.

"One of the neighbors could call the cops," Gianni says. "If you're out here to see them coming, you can call and warn us. We'll slip out the back, meet you over one block."

"You want a lookout, you shoulda brought one."

Gianni wags his head, showing her how stupid he thinks she's acting, but he snaps open his door, comes around to pop the shotgun side for Mama Bones. Gianni's three guys followed in another car, but they parked a street over. They're all going to meet in the trees near Ryder's front door.

"I'm getting another hunch," Mama Bones says.

"About what? I'd better start paying attention to these hunches."

"Big shoes."

"Shoes?"

"I show you later. Maybe. If I'm right."

Mama Bones holds her Sig Sauer tucked against her belly. They walk casually on the opposite sidewalk before ducking across the highway and into Ryder's front yard forest. Heck, the place probably has more trees than the Everglades, and these pines, spruce and fir trees are so much taller. They can see pretty good because the evergreens don't stop all the light, but they still take five minutes to get through, hook up with Gianni's men. Takes another five minutes to check the security system and get a guy inside to open the doors.

Mama Bones tip-toes down Barbara Ryder's first-floor hardwood hall, the last one of the single file group, the muzzle of her Sig Sauer aimed almost straight down. Both of her palms squeeze the gun grips. Both of her thumbs are together and pointing forward. But her trigger finger waits, pointing straight out along the frame above the guard. Domenic taught her good. You don't touch triggers until you're ready to shoot.

Somebody is close to her. The hair on her neck straightens.

"Dustin's pretty sure no one's home," Gianni whispers.

Mama Bones jumps, her shoulders, arms and hands flinching. Gianni lead them inside. She thought he was still up front. But he came back into Barbara Ryder's hallway from her left side, startled her. Checking out houses is a lot harder than those TV cop shows make it seem. You gotta go *slow*.

"But you said the cars are still here," Mama Bones says. "Even Austin's. Did you send somebody in back to check the boat dock?"

"Boat dock? Oh, crap."

Mama Bones spreads her palm against Gianni's chest, pushes him away and goes to look for the master suite. She watched a movie last summer that made her laugh, but now she's figuring what happened in that movie could be the answer to all her questions about the missing ex-mayor Croc Tierney and Ryder.

She finds the master suite upstairs, the big bedroom, sitting room, double baths and the two giant walk-in closets, one of them empty. Two big windows look out on the backyard flower garden, the boat dock with Gianni's men on it, and sparkling lights from other multi-million-dollar estates across the river.

She flips a switch. Overhead chandeliers throw light on pale blue and white bedcovers, a French lilies pattern that matches designs on the drapes and the thick carpeting. First day she met Barbara Ryder, Mama

Bones knew the woman had class. Mama Bones also noticed her big nose and big feet.

The walk-in closets hide behind cedar doors near the shower. On one side of the full closet is a long rack of dresses, skirts and blouses. On the opposite side, another rack holds men's suits, sport coats and trousers. On the men's shelf are clear-wrapped packages of clean dress shirts. Women's sweaters fill the opposite shelf. And on the floor, men's shoes line up neatly beneath the suits, women's shoes under the dresses.

Mama Bones lifts a pair of women's strapped white pumps, *Diane Lynns*, and slips her two longest fingers inside. Then from across the closet she picks up a pair of men's black wingtips, does the same, measuring the length. Measuring the size.

She holds both pairs up in the light to make sure. All four shoes are the same size. Big. She was right. Croc Tierney and Barbara Ryder are the same person, kinda like that old movie she saw last summer, *Victor, Victoria.*

NINETEEN

It's after midnight when Gianni tells Mama Bones the search at Ryder's is over. She asks, so he brings the car all the way down the long driveway, stops right in front of Ryder's big front door. None of the neighbors is paying attention. Nobody's watching. And Mama Bones is tired, ready to climb in her bed and sleep.

She sighs sitting next to her nephew in the air-conditioned Cadillac Escalade, disappointed about not finding Austin, but cooler. It's a hot night, even near the water. Smarty Pants talked himself out of lots of scrapes over the years. And he's not stupid, knows when it's time to make a move, the big mouth bond salesman showing plenty of guts when he needed to shoot a hole in the Turk. Saved her life, kinda.

Maybe he'll make it.

But if Mama Bones has things figured right—that Barbara Ryder and her long-missing, fugitive ex-mayor brother Steven Crocodile Tierney are the same person— then poor old Smarty Pants is almost surely already dead. Probably feeding the crabs at the bottom of the Navasquan River.

It's his own fault, thinking with the wrong head, letting his you-know-what talk him into hanging out with that mamaluke Emma Tierney again. Austin acts like her own horny son Vic—like lots of dumb men do all their lives. And this trip, for Smarty Pants, the irresistible redhead brought Austin straight to The Grim Reaper, Emma's papa, Croc Tierney, alias Barbara Ryder, who from now on—so Mama Bones don't get confused—she's gonna call the ex-mayor. That morally corrupt, public-money stealing, fugitive horse-player won't waste a minute getting rid of Austin Carr. Too bad. She was beginning to make plans for Austin.

Gianni pulls away from Ryder's house before Mama Bones gets her shoulder-harness hooked. Her fingers are stiff and numb like bird claws. When she finally gets the belt latch hooked, she says, "How come you and Dustin are so sure they all left in a boat, huh?"

"The cars are there. The people aren't."

Mama Bones shrugs. "They could have been picked up by another car before you had a guy out front."

"Maybe, but the boat dock is active, set up for the Grand Banks that isn't there anymore. The dock ropes are loose, and there's fresh wear on the foam guards. Also, Dustin's guy is pretty sure he heard a boat engine this evening."

"Now he tells us?"

Gianni shrugs. "It was me didn't know there was a boat dock. I didn't tell anybody to watch the river."

The moon and stars are hidden from her again on the dark Rumson street. She'd like to be quiet the rest of the ride home because it's hard for her not to think about Austin trying to breathe underwater and pieces of Tomas in a wheelbarrow. But she wants to know what her nephew thinks.

"Maybe Austin could still be alive if we find the boat, huh?" she asks.

"With his mouth, there's always a chance," Gianni says. "I knew Bluefish's man Max, the stone killer Austin Carr talked into being his chauffeur. That stockbroker could charm a snake. But if Ryder left an hour before we went inside, and you add on the time we took to find paperwork on the Grand Banks, get a man to the Sea Bright bridge...Croc and them could be twenty miles from shore, in the open Atlantic Ocean, on their way anywhere in the world."

"Or docked a mile away," Mama Bones says. "Zip Your Lip's big race is tomorrow."

"We have a hundred eyes on the river, and we'll have a hundred more when the sun comes up."

"That could be too late."

"It's probably already too late," Gianni says. "Why keep Austin alive? If Croc's dumb enough to hang around, actually come to the track to watch the race tomorrow, he wouldn't want Austin with him."

"If the ex-mayor and his daughter left hours ago, how are they gonna know we or anybody else is onto them?"

"For one thing," Gianni says, "Croc's partner Turk was murdered. So were Turk's two friendly cops. His crew sure knows something bad happened."

"Okay, but how could the ex-mayor know I figured out the twin horse angle? He and Turk's men might run the scam anyway, try to collect."

"Maybe it's time to call my FBI contact," Gianni says, "tell her about Ryder and the boat. Get their help searching."

Mama Bones shakes her head. "Tell her about everything *but* the boat. Tell her maybe Barbara Ryder is really Croc, not Croc's sister. That Zip Your Lip is a phony, a twin and that she's running tomorrow. We want the FBI at the track, but not on the boat until we find out if Austin's alive."

Mama Bones wakes in her warm bed next day listening to Gianni walk the stairs and her hallway with happy feet. Quick and certain. Not sluggish, even though he's carrying something—probably coffee. Why so eager, huh? She can only hope and pray.

He knocks.

She pushes herself up against the headboard and wraps her shoulders with the shawl that always hangs from the bedpost beside her. "Come on in, Gianni. What's the good news, huh?"

"We found the boat," he says.

The steam coming off the espresso he sets on her nightstand smells like that sidewalk restaurant she and Domenic found by the Colosseum in Rome. That same anniversary trip. The young couple who owned the restaurant were so nice.

"The ex-mayor's docked at that little V.I.P. pier behind the racetrack," Gianni says.

"I thought that corporate perk got closed when the state took over?"

Gianni shrugs. "It did. But Turk must have fixed it with the commission before he died. The Grand Banks is docked there this morning. Get dressed if you want to come find out if Austin's still alive."

Mama Bones sips her espresso. "Did you call the FBI?"

"Yup. She says they'll be at the track. If Croc or Ryder show, he...she...the ex-mayor will be arrested."

"You didn't tell her about the boat?"

"Not yet."

I'm jammed in a solid wooden box, some tiny portion of the boat's below-deck spaces devoted to storage. A very tiny part. Tied up, gagged, barely able to breathe through my nose, I—the ever-cool big mouth—battle each and every second not to flip out and asphyxiate myself with sheer terror. I focus on my temporary helplessness, believing the one and only possibility of survival lies in meditation to conquer the fear. I choose the subject dearest my heart to concentrate on, the people whose faces and love carried me through this unpredictable and vicious world.

The redheaded women I've slept with.

I'm kidding.

Not easy thing to do under the circumstances—joke—but people who know me count on one thing from Austin Carr: silly. It must be genetic, past generations of Carrs having earned their keep through mirth, an offer of relief and distraction from the everyday horrors of human tribal life.

I really was kidding about the redheaded women. I'm like most fathers, pushing back the panic by remembering each and every thing I can about my two children—Elizabeth, my oldest, and Ryan, Beth's younger brother by three years. The hospital experiences at each birth consumed the first ten or twenty minutes of this boat ride—what I now call The Croc and Emma Tierney hijacking. Beth and Ryan's toddler episodes were next, including the time Beth gave Aunt Dee a hickey on her forehead, latching on with her lips until Aunt Dee's skin went purple. The kids' first two dozen birthday parties are currently on my playlist, all the different places Susan and I took a pack of our kids' friends. Chucky Cheese and the local bowling alley were hits.

Footsteps.

On a dead end street one hundred yards from Seaside Park's stable area, Mama Bones struggles to focus the binoculars Gianni handed over. She or her nephew is blind like a bat. Hard to say which, the controls are so far off. Another cup of espresso might have helped. This is too early for Mama Bones to be up, especially after being out so late the night before. It's funny how much she hopes Austin is still alive. Maybe it's Vic being back in the hospital, or Tomas getting killed that makes her worry too much about the stockbroker. But Smarty Pants also saved her life shooting Turk.

Not kinda, either. Definitely.

Mama Bones finally zooms in on the ex-mayor's boat through an oblong hole in the privet hedge. Wood-framed, two-bedroom ranch houses sit on either side of the bulk-headed inlet, the piece of water no bigger than a large swimming pool. Both houses have back lawns that slope down to the water on either side of the white yacht, the dock floating between the homes like a big toy. A parking space for two cars is the inlet's third bulkhead border, its broken asphalt tucked between the tiny inlet and the privet hedge Mama Bones peeks through.

"You're right." Mama Bones says. "Somebody's moving inside the boat cabin."

Something bumps the storage box I'm stuffed inside. The yacht's polished wood vibrates through my bones like the tug of a spider checking her web, and I pray to an unknown Higher Power the movement signals the end of my confinement. One way or another: freedom or death, I care not which. My meditations are failing. A cold-sweat of fear engulfs my soul through widening cracks of despair.

The lid comes off my cage and the cramped black torture explodes with light and hope. I blink and squint a few seconds before I recognize the person standing over me. It's Emma Tierney with a bloody face. Her cheek is slashed and bruised. The eye above is closed with purple swelling.

My heart bumps up to a steady drumroll when I see Emma's right hand holds a serrated steak knife. Her fingertips shine white with the pressure of squeezing the blade's plain wooden handle. I worry she's going to stab me, but her free hand rips the sticky tape from my mouth instead.

I suck in fresh air. "Thank God, Emma." My voice is odd, childlike. "Thank you."

"Hold your hands up," she whispers. "And hold them still. Hurry."

She uses her knife to saw the tape wrapping my wrists. She's in hurry, barely taking enough time to avoid slicing my flesh, glancing over her shoulder at an adjoining private cabin. New bruises mark both of her arms and wrists, and I notice she's wearing only a white slip. It's smooth and worn, maybe silk. Along the lace neckline there's a smudge of fresh blood.

I grip the edge of the box I'm inside and try to push-pull myself out, but my arms can't manage my full weight. My legs are numb with inactivity and being cramped. Only with Emma's help do I manage to even fall outside the coffin-like container.

I'm pulling the tape off my ankles when Emma's tormentor runs into the cabin. I don't know what else to call him. Or her. Or it, an in-between or a both. The sex part doesn't matter. Croc or Barbara. What's important is the predator part, the violence; one human physically and mentally abusing another for personal gratification.

That's how I see it anyway, although it's quite possible my intense distaste for the ex-mayor could be affected by his re-appearance. See, Croc Tierney is stark naked when he runs into the cabin. And it's even worse than that, if you know what I mean. He's clearly a male, and he's...uh...excited.

It's disgusting what he's apparently done to his own

daughter, besides beating her, I mean. Plus, for me and I think a majority of heterosexual men, there are few things more distasteful to observe than another man's erect penis.

Head down, scrambling to remove the tape from my ankles, I throw up a teaspoon of stomach bile. What a world. There should be a special kind of penalty for a guy who rapes his daughter. I get the tape off and struggle to my knees, then stand to fend off the naked streaker. But Croc is not after me.

Emma keeps her back to Croc until he grabs her arm and raises his other fist to punch her. The horror and shock of the scene are almost too much for me—a man beating a woman, his nakedness and arousal, the frailty of Emma in her underwear. It's hard to deal with the disgust and anger prodding me into action. I've overwhelmed with rage and impotence, unable to move, unable to save the helpless woman.

But Emma chooses that perfect moment to spin and deliver the point of her knife to her father's exposed chest. There's fury in her motion, the twist and the thrust of her weapon blurred by what I imagine to be years of torture and abuse. Her lips are curled in terror and temper, her eyes glassy with moisture.

Emma screams as the jagged blade slides to the hilt between the ex-mayor's ribs, her attack level with his breast bone. She must be driving that blade very close— if not into—Tierney's beating heart.

He opens his mouth to gasp, but no sound escapes. He goes limp as he falls.

Gianni and Mama Bones scamper down into the cabin.

TWENTY

A week later Gianni welcomes me inside Mama Bones' house, Gianni all fresh and cool in a new Tommy Bahama camp shirt, this one peach-colored with white hibiscus. Though dapper and handsome, Gianni is not invited for dinner; this I know because when he shows me into the dining room, only two settings of silver and china decorate the linen-covered table.

Mama Bones called yesterday to make sure the FBI was done with me, said I should come over tonight for lasagna, settle up our business. Judging by the way this dining room is decorated and arranged, I'm guessing Mama Bones might have something more of a celebration on her mind. There's French Champagne chilling in a silver bucket.

Gianni turns to leave. "Mama Bones is on the telephone. She said to make sure you had a drink. There's red wine or sambuca on the table." He points.

"What about the Champagne?"

"Maybe later," he says.

I hear Mama Bones in the next room, talking to her son Vic on the phone. She's talking loud, pretty excited that he's being released this weekend. I try not to eavesdrop any more than I already have, so I tour the dining room. Photographs in all sizes and shapes fill every table, bookshelf cranny and window ledge. To me there's something warm and touching about a house loaded with family pictures. Not a shrine to one or two kids, a dead husband, but all kinds of children and fathers, aunts and uncles, babies and great grandmothers, laughing and posing, most growing older over time.

Minutes later Mama Bones carries in a silver tray of calamari. There's enough battered and deep-fried hollow rings of fresh squid to feed a basketball team—pounds of the stuff, piled so high she has to peer around it. "Hello, Smarty Pants. I see you put on clean blue jeans for me."

Mama Bones is all Jersey. A chop buster, born and raised. "My tux is at the cleaners. I didn't know it was Champagne night."

She places the tray of calamari in the center of the dining table, wraps her arms around me and busses my cheek with her lips. I hug her in return, kissing mostly her ear. We're practically a team, Mama Bones and I. Like me and Luis. We keep saving each other.

She says, "Plenty of time for our business. First sit down and drink some wine."

"The stock and bond business, right? Bonacelli Investments?"

"Sure. But sit down, have a drink first. You're a guest in my house."

Mama Bones takes the head of the table, the only chair with arms. To be fair, it's also the spot nearest the kitchen, and I know food is going to be a big part of the night. I've eaten her lasagna, too. It's killer. The woman could be a championship chef if she wasn't the Shore's biggest bookie.

She pours us both a glass of wine from a decanter. "Did you talk to the expectant father Luis before he took off to Mexico?"

I take the seat on her left, my back to the parlor, my gaze on Mama Bones and the open doorway into her sunny kitchen. It's still bright at seven in the evening. "Yeah. I called him this afternoon on his boat's ship-to-shore. Rosalinda's doing better, he says. Probably the idea of going home, seeing her daughters."

Mama Bones nods. "She has to be a mother for her children. It will force her to deal with her husband's death. I remember."

I chug my glass of wine, recalling the way Rosalinda's husband Heriberto looked at me before Turk shot him barely two months ago. Pitiful. Begging for my help. I hated being helpless that night. I still feel helpless now, even though I killed the Turk. Maybe it's because I shot him in the back.

Mama Bones refills my wine glass from a two-liter glass jug. Though cheap, it's not a bad tasting wine. It's all Mama Bone drinks. A generic and mislabeled Burgundy from one of California's largest wine producers.

"So Vic just called," she says. "He's gonna get out of the hospital this weekend. With Carmela's help, he should be able to run Bonacelli Investments okay. You don't have to worry about that business no more."

I nod. Not much to say. Honestly, I'm having ambiguous feelings about leaving the stock and bond game, but it's what I need to do.

"You know what you gonna do after?" she asks.

"No, not really. I've made some money the last few years—a finder's fee from the insurance company, the profit from that insider trading deal with Patricia Willis I got to keep, plus what I expect my percentage of Bonacelli Investments is worth now. I don't have to rush into anything. Maybe I should write a book about Croc Tierney and his daughter. I've already been called by two literary agents."

"Are they gonna prosecute Emma?" Mama Bones ask.

"Not for killing her father. At least that's what her attorney thinks. But they haven't decided on kidnapping charges. I downplayed Emma's role, but Zimmer reminded me I didn't want to actually lie to Federal agents."

"She got a good lawyer?"

"Very good. Her real estate company is standing up for her. Plus, she's a big producer, has some money of her own."

"She's been through a lot."

"No kidding. But she knows it. Her attorney wanted to arrange new therapy before any trial starts, and she's agreed."

"That's good. So, I got two checks for you under that dinner plate." She points.

I lift my antique china. The first check is made out to me in the amount of three hundred thousand dollars. The second check is a duplicate of the first except for the amount: this one's for half a million.

I sputter. "What...why?"

Mama Bones spears a golden ring of calamari with her three-pronged salad fork. "The three hundred thousand is for your share of Bonacelli Investments. You still wanna get out, right?"

"I do, and that's very generous. It's ten times what I paid for the stock two years ago."

"You, Vic and Carmela did a heck of a job turning the place around. And the number is fair. It's based on eight times the past year's earnings. A little on the high side. You think the check's too big, rip it up, I'll write you a new one. How about two-fifty?"

I throw up my hands, spilling my wine. Guess I'm a little excited. Not that I'm a man driven by greed. I'm just practical. My children's educations were already covered with zero coupon bonds, but now I can help with graduate school or starting a business. Plus I can buy new golf clubs. I'm going to be semi-rich.

Mama Bones throws her napkin on the wine I spilled. "My tablecloth's gonna have a stain."

I decide to drink more, see if additional consumption calms me down. I pour myself another glass of unspecified grapes and vintages. With checks here totaling eight hundred thousand dollars, I could soon afford much better wine—even the imported stuff. Lots of zeroes on these checks. Lucky I haven't fainted yet.

"What's the second check for?" I say.

"Let's call that one a signing bonus. It's really more like your retirement, because—you know—once you're in, you don't get out."

"Excuse me?"

"You only get that check if you say yes to my other proposal. So let's call it a signing bonus."

"One more time, slowly. In detail."

"Okay." Mama Bones stabs two more calamari rings, puts them on her plate. "You should try this. You don't like squid or something?"

I transfer a scoop to my plate. "Love it."

"The thing is, I got a temporary promotion. I have new duties that could go on for a long time, hopefully longer than Turk's reign. Vic will handle the investments. But I need you to help with the homeless women I've been collecting. I didn't know I'd have to step into...uh, my new role."

"Wait. You want me to work for you? You're asking me to join the Mafia?"

Mama Bones gives me a rare toothy grin. "No, no. You work for me like a personal assistant. Or a gardener, huh? Like Gianni a little because you have to stay in touch with me all the time, only you have nothing to do with...the family business. Heck, me and Gianni don't do much with New York people either."

"I don't understand."

"Forget all that," she says. "That's got nothing to do with you. With me taking the Turk's job, I'm not gonna have enough time for the women I've agreed to help. And neither is Gianni."

"What exactly would I do?"

Mama Bones smiles. "You gonna manage the motel I just bought to house the women and their kids—run the books anyway—and also you work with Luis and Solana on bringing orphaned Mexican kids to New York to see a good doctor. Sometimes we find a family for them after."

"Luis showed me a picture of the orphanage where he and Rosalinda lived. He finally told me about your connection."

"That's nice. So specifically, you gonna stay in touch with all kinds of people in Arizona, Texas, California, Mexico and Jersey, plus shift money around," Mama Bones says. "Telephone work, pretty much, except maybe once in a while you and Luis might have to make a trip on his boat."

"You make it sound easy. Too easy for half a million signing bonus."

Mama Bones sniffs. "Remember it's really your retirement up front. You're a fairly young man. I expect you to work for me a long time. But I'm not gonna kid you. You're not gonna be in the Mafia, but you might see and hear stuff, and if you take my money, you're on the Mama Bones ship, you know. Maybe...we could sink."

I dip three crispy circles of squid into the red sauce, pop them in my mouth. Those checks and Mama Bones' offer tempt me. I would love to do something important with the rest of my life, something more consequential than helping fund state and local governments with tax-free debt they don't want to pay back. Honestly, I had no idea Mama Bones thought me so capable.

"The new women's home will be your biggest job, although you're gonna have no contact with the women. Other trained women professionals are going to run the place. Father Ignacio has many friends. What I did, I bought an old motel on Highway 35. You gotta fix it up, acting like a general contractor, and then run the facility's books when it's ready—pay the bills, handle everything. It's thirty-six beds."

"Thirty-six beds? That's a big motel. Who's paying for this?"

"Me. I got special accounts set up—different limited liability corporations. LLCs."

"Do I get any fancy titles? I always liked a good title."

"Sure, if you want. How do you like President of Angelina's School of Charm?"

"Got any others?"

"You get a salary of one hundred ten thousand a year."

I chew on the squid. Something like this, you have to say yes or no right away. Mama Bones isn't going to like it if I ask for time to consider. Besides that, I'm not sure I need time. I said I wanted out of the securities business. No more cold calls. No more defaulted bonds, stock market crashes and financial disasters. No more disappointed, unhappy clients.

No more bullets!

This money sets me and my kids for life, too, if I invest well. I'm not sure what I'll be telling Mama Bones' contacts on the telephone, but it sounds safe enough. Besides, anything I do will be less violent than my recent experiences as a stockbroker.

"I want to get away from the violence," I say. "Are you sure I won't be part of...you know...any family operations? No criminal work, right?"

"Absolutely not. You handle my charity stuff, legal business only."

"Okay, I'll do it. I'm your man."

"That's great. I know you gonna like being part of my team." She reaches for the Champagne, then changes her mind, points at my checks. Man that's a lot of zeroes. "I'll make sure that money gets in my account right away. For sure by next week."

Huh?

"And now," she says, "I got a gift for you."

I figure she means the bubbling wine, but no. She removes a gray plastic carry-case from the sideboard drawer. The rectangular box is about the size of a telephone book, but heavier, and has a blue ribbon wrapped across opposing corners, a greeting card tucked under the ribbon. My name is printed on the card.

"Welcome to the family," the card says.

I remove the ribbon and open the case. The container splits lengthwise, and a half-inch thick instruction booklet falls to the table beside the calamari. The first words I read on the booklet's cover are, "A stainless steel barrel requires less maintenance and is corrosion resistant, perfectly suited for concealment close to active, perspiring bodies."

My gift from Mama Bones is a fifteen-shot Sig Sauer .45, a factory-new semiautomatic pistol.

ABOUT THE AUTHOR

Former Los Angeles Times reporter Jack Getze is Fiction Editor for Anthony nominated Spinetingler Magazine. Through the Los Angeles Times/Washington Post News Syndicate, his news and feature stories have been published in over five-hundred newspapers and periodicals worldwide. His screwball mysteries, BIG NUMBERS and BIG MONEY, were first published by Hilliard Harris in 2007 and 2008. His short stories have appeared in *A Twist of Noir* and *Beat to a Pulp*. He is an Active Member of Mystery Writers of America's New York Chapter.

http://austincarrscrimediary.blogspot.com/

OTHER TITLES FROM DOWN AND OUT BOOKS

See www.DownAndOutBooks.com for complete list

By William Hastings (editor)
*Stray Dogs: Writing from the
Other America*

By Matt Hilton
No Going Back
Rules of Honor
The Lawless Kind (*)

By Terry Holland
An Ice Cold Paradise
Chicago Shiver

By Darrel James,
Linda O. Johnston &
Tammy Kaehler (editors)
Last Exit to Murder

By David Housewright &
Renée Valois
The Devil and the Diva

By David Housewright
Finders Keepers
Full House

By Jon & Ruth Jordan (editors)
Murder and Mayhem in Muskego
Cooking with Crimespree

By Andrew McAleer &
Paul D. Marks (editors)
Coast to Coast (*)

By Bill Moody
Czechmate
The Man in Red Square

Solo Hand
The Death of a Tenor Man
The Sound of the Trumpet
Bird Lives!

By Gary Phillips
The Perpetrators
Scoundrels (Editor)
Treacherous

By Robert J. Randisi
Upon My Soul
Souls of the Dead
Envy the Dead (*)

By Ryan Sayles
The Subtle Art of Brutality
Warpath (*)

By Anthony Neil Smith
Worm

By Liam Sweeny
Welcome Back, Jack (*)

By Art Taylor (editor)
*Murder Under the Oaks:
Bouchercon Anthology 2015* (*)

By Lono Waiwaiole
Wiley's Lament
Wiley's Shuffle
Wiley's Refrain
Dark Paradise

By Vincent Zandri
Moonlight Weeps

(*)—Coming Soon